Surgeon's Call

by

Elizabeth Harrison

Dales Large Print Books
Long Preston, North Yorkshire,
BD23 4ND, England.

British Library Cataloguing in Publication Data.

Harrison, Elizabeth
  Surgeon's call.

  A catalogue record of this book is
  available from the British Library

  ISBN 978-1-84262-580-4 pbk

Cover illustration by arrangement with
P.W.A. International Ltd.

The moral right of the author has been asserted

Published in Large Print 2008 by arrangement with
Elizabeth Harrison, care of Watson, Little Ltd.

Dales Large Print is an imprint of Library Magna Books Ltd.

Printed and bound in Great Britain by
T.J. (International) Ltd., Cornwall, PL28 8RW

Contents

Prologue in Nepal

Tall, long-legged and narrow-hipped, Michael Adversane was one of the best-looking of the young surgeons at the Central London Hospital, and easily the most elegant – though it would be difficult to recognize this now, as he stood in the airport in jeans, sweater, anorak, rucksack at his feet, a scruffy pair of plimsolls donned for comfort on the long flight. Normally, though, his trendy gear set Central fashion – his shirts flowered and ruffled, his dark hair longer than anyone but an Adversane would dare.

He had been born in Harley Street, the grandson of Sir Frederick Adversane, that eminent and distinguished physician, and Lady Adversane, herself a world figure in biochemistry. Michael, making a reputation for himself not only in surgery but as a mountaineer, was already marked out for the almost instant success expected from his family.

A tall, erect figure, white-haired now, with the brilliant blue eyes her grandson had inherited, Lady Adversane had come to the airport to see him off. Jane was with her, a red-haired student with a casual air, overlaid this morning by misery. Jane always hated good-byes. Her mouth quivered, the soft brown eyes filled.

Michael kissed them both, patted Jane reassuringly. 'Cheer up, I'll be home before you've noticed I'm gone.'

Nothing could be further from the truth, and she sniffed dolefully, produced a fragile, wavering smile.

He would be away for four months, when he returned would become Resident Surgical Officer at the Central London Hospital, the most coveted surgical appointment there before a consultancy. Once he had taken on the post, though, he'd be in for two years of all-demanding surgery, of broken nights, of living at the end of the telephone, responsible for every admission on the surgical side.

At present the exhilaration that came at the outset of a mountain holiday gripped him. Setting off for the unknown, with rucksack and sleeping bag, the sense of adventure, of a new world opening, always came to him like a gift from the gods. On this occasion, too, it was indeed the unknown – unclimbed peaks in the Himalayas. Rupert Fiske, who was leading the expedition, had been thankful to learn that Michael, who combined both medical knowledge and mountaineering experience, could spare the time to join him.

In Katmandu they met, and Michael was

introduced to the remaining members of the party. Their supplies – shipped months earlier from Southampton – had been brought on from Bombay by Rupert and Johnnie Exton, nineteen and the youngest in the group that was now to fly on together in an ancient Dakota to an airstrip where goats came meandering curiously around their packing cases, while water buffalo chewed phlegmatically on the perimeter. Here they had to transfer themselves and their belongings to the shabby little plane that would take them on the next stage of the journey.

Six flights, in fact, were needed to move the stores, and Michael, who was to travel on the final trip, sat meanwhile in the grass-roofed hut, all that the airstrip possessed by way of a terminal, writing his final letters home. One to his grandmother. This would be the last she could hear of him for three months – though it required an act of faith on his part to believe that any letter could find its way from this field deep in Nepal to the house in Harley Street. Another to Rachel, of course. Beautiful Rachel of the huge eyes and the air of frailty that had first drawn her to him. One letter followed by three months silence would strain her devotion, he thought ruefully. The call of the Himalayas had been strong, but he couldn't help wondering if he might not be pushing his luck too far, leaving Rachel alone in

London. Julian Northcott in particular had always had an eye for her.

Time in hand still, so he began another letter, an impulse, he was to feel later, that might well have saved his life. A letter to his former chief on the orthopedic unit, Sir Alexander Drummond, Jane's father. With a sudden memory of Jane battling fiercely with her tears, he enclosed a brief note for her, too. A pity she had not been able to come to Nepal with him. But her climbing experience, though far from negligible – Michael had taught her himself on alpine holidays – was not up to this sort of expedition. Moreover, in her final year as a medical student, she could hardly have spared four months away from the Central.

He was to miss her often as they crossed the open moorlands of grass and peat, where small lost villages showed him a side of medicine unknown today back in the Central. Here were diseases hardly seen at home, and the limited supply of drugs he had been able to bring with him was in constant demand, while he worked at his village surgeries as intensively as he had done in outpatients. This was when he wished most for Jane, of course. Another pair of trained hands would have been invaluable – and the experience would have been as enlightening to her as it was to him. Now and again he encountered short and reasonably satisfying cases – a wound to dress, a bone to set, an abscess to incise and drain. But these small successes were nothing, compared with the numbers he was forced to turn away. The nearest X ray and microscope were out of reach, and often he could do no more than advise the patient to visit the hospital in the nearest town, several weeks march away. Typhoid, malaria, tuberculosis, goiter, severe chronic anemias and, above all, malnutrition, surrounded him. With the best will in the world, there was often nothing he could do for this population, at risk from epidemics, food shortages and debilitating chronic disease. In these Himalayan villages, the life expectancy of the average man was no more than thirty-five years – less than it had been in Chaucer's England.

Medical problems apart, the journey of two hundred miles across the plains and into the lush green forests of the foothills was easy and carefree. With the temperature in the seventies, they crossed flowery meadows, passed through thickets of rhododendron, finally established a base camp among birches and azaleas. Round them now the panorama of snow-covered peaks, unexplored, unclimbed.

Now, too, as birch forest gave way to heather and glacial moraines, the arduous real climbing began at last. They left their porters, had to carry on their backs all they were going to need. Here in the high Himalayas, body and spirit were stretched to the limit. Life was hard, skill and stamina a necessity for survival. Each man depended on his neighbour, a mistake could cost a life. Teamwork became instinctive.

They were nearing the point when they hoped to be able to make the final assault on the peak they had come so far to climb. They were confronted by stark, seemingly impassable cliffs of sculptured ice falling to glaciers thousands of feet below, cutting them off effectively from the peak they had imagined to be so near. Before they could begin the final assault they had to descend these icy cliffs, cross the glaciers, then regain the height they had lost. There was no alternative. Slowly and cautiously they explored, until eventually they succeeded in finding a route down the precipitous mountainside. Once on the glaciers, ibex with great horns spanning three feet stared at them, while game was inquisitive and unafraid. Man came as a stranger to them all. Here the hunters they knew were eagles and the snow leopard.

The small party crossed the glacier, began the long climb upwards. Two weeks had been devoured in the descent. If the monsoons held off, though, they might still have time to reach the summit. Now the weather had become their enemy, and the season was against them. Their luck was out. The monsoons came early, and they began to hear the rumble and thunder of distant avalanches. A perilous and unnerving sound. That extra fortnight had been fatal.

Here on the roof of Asia they were isolated. If trouble came they would have to find their own way out of it. They had no means of contacting the outside world, no search party could have found them. If their return were delayed too long they would begin to run short of food. All they needed, Michael thought, was for a storm to immobilize them in their tents twenty thousand feet up the mountainside. Then their diet would be in real danger. As it was, until they reached the base camp again, they would be on restricted rations.

Rupert took the decision, the peak less than a week's climb away, to turn back. Common sense demanded it, and they knew him to be right. Even so, they were discouraged as they began the descent, gloom took over as they had to concede victory to the mountain they could see so clearly.

This, though, was climbing. This was what it was about. Never easy, and triumphs few, hard won. The attempt had been worthwhile, none of them were sorry to have made it. Another year they would return again.

Michael was on the end of the rope, Johnnie Exton above him, when suddenly the danger they had heard in the distance for so long was upon them. There were urgent calls from above, and looking up, he could see a great soft avalanche tumbling like some vast billowing cloud ready to engulf them. He yelled furiously to Johnnie to fling himself sideways into the shelter of the overhanging rock, pressed himself hard against the icy cliff, tried to hold fast. This, he thought for a fleeting moment of fatalism, this is the end – the end of mountaineering, the end of surgery.

Compressed air buffeted him, snow blinded him, chips of ice cut through thick layers of clothing into his flesh like razors. A vast hand seemed to tug at his shoulders, and he fought it, but knew the rucksack torn from his back, then his body from its desperate hold.

He found himself sprawled half across eternity, his rucksack a thousand feet below. He was lucky not to be there himself. His legs were torn and bleeding, one doubled ominously beneath him. But the avalanche had passed, and he was here, alive. Slowly he inched his way back to safety. Encouraging shouts told him help was on its way.

Waves of pain and nausea hit him with each difficult movement, and as soon as he reached a position of minimum safety he lay still. Soon kind hands and calm voices took charge. He was able to relax briefly, slip away into oblivion.

'He's passed out,' Rupert said to Johnnie. 'Just as well.' They looked at one another with bleak determination, and Johnnie gestured downwards, where the rucksack, a distant speck, could still be seen. It held the bulk of their medical supplies.

'We must do what we can,' Rupert said. 'First of all we must somehow get him to the base camp. When he comes around he'll be able to advise us himself about his injuries, of course.'

The journey was to take many hard weeks, and when the exhausted little party reached the plains their patient was nearing the end of his resources. The roughly set and crudely splinted fractures in his injured leg had taken a battering, the leg was bruised and infected. From the base camp, they sent runners on ahead. In the market town where nearly four months earlier they had set off, the shabby little plane awaited them. It took off chaotically as ever, but came safely down on the familiar airstrip among the water buffalo and the ambling goats, where to Rupert's relief the Dakota and its pilot stood ready for them.

Someone else was ready, too.

Michael thought he must be in extreme delirium, his fever worse than he'd known. Incredible. Ridiculous. He screwed his eyes up skeptically.

But the bulky reassuring figure remained there, was bending over him, while the kindly unflurried tones he had so often heard in the wards were for him now.

'Well, Mike, you seem to have got yourself into a bit of a sorry state, I must say. We shall have to see what we can do about it.'

Sandy Drummond, from the Central London Hospital. Here, unbelievingly, in Nepal.

1

The Central London Hospital

'Have you heard about Sandy Drummond?' they were asking at the Central. 'He's dropped everything and flown out to Katmandu after his former registrar – apparently Adversane's gone and fallen off a mountain or something. Anyway, Sandy's got the breeze up.'

'Sandy's not normally alarmist.'

'No. They say old Lady Adversane had a cable, telephoned Sandy about it. He rang Katmandu himself, didn't like the answers they gave him, and cancelled his appointments right and left. His secretary rang around B.O.A.C., Air India, the Foreign Office and the Nepalese Embassy. Sandy handed his ward over to Leo Rosenstein, somehow succeeded in extracting Sister Henderson from the General Theater – don't ask me how he managed it – and took off for the Himalayas with her.'

'I don't care for it at all,' Sandy had explained to Lord Mummery, the senior surgeon. 'By all reports, it's three weeks now since the avalanche that did all the damage.

19

It's going to be four weeks at least before they can get young Mike into the hospital in Katmandu. And what sort of shape is he going to be in by then?'

'What treatment has he had so far, have you heard?'

'Only what he's been fit enough to prescribe for himself. He's the expedition's doctor, after all. They've no other medical man with them. It's not exactly good country for moving people about on stretchers, either. As far as I can gather, it's a case of get off and crawl around the worst bits.

Mummery frowned. 'Must say, I agree with you. I don't like the sound of it.'

'No. What's more, they're short of drugs. Most of their medical supplies were lost in the avalanche. The two members of the party Fiske sent on ahead to alert the Dakota and the hospital authorities particularly stressed that they were out of antibiotics.'

'Infection in the fractures, you think, then?'

'Almost inevitable in the circumstances, wouldn't you say, Basil? I'm getting out there without waiting for a hospital report on his condition. My presence can do no harm, and may possibly achieve something useful.'

At the Central they said afterwards that Sandy's prompt departure had saved Mike Adversane's life. Even so, it was a mere shadow of the Adversane they knew who was admitted by ambulance from the airport to the side room on Ambroise Paré ward in the Central three weeks later. Emaciated, feverish, and with a leg that worried them all.

'When I set eyes on him I knew I'd been right to go out there. He had an open infected fracture, in a limb with a badly reduced blood supply. At first I thought there was nothing for it but to take it off then and there, in the Dakota, with only a young Nepalese house surgeon and Sister Henderson to assist me,' Sandy told Leo Rosenstein. 'Fortunately, though, it didn't come to that. When we had given him some blood and loaded him with antibiotics, I was able to work on the fractures, and I came to the conclusion there was still a chance of saving the leg, so we did what we could.' He sighed. 'But here we have this infected and barely visible limb. Are we going to be able to salvage it? I don't know. I daren't forecast.'

They did their best – and at the Central their best was very good indeed – but finally Sandy had to put it to Michael without evasion.

'You know,' he said, sitting down by Michael's bed in his misleadingly placid manner, 'I don't honestly think this is going to get right. Not with the blood supply so impaired. To be frank with you, I doubt if its

21

remediable.' Sandy was trying to disguise it, but distress lay heavily on him. In his sixties now, though an energetic and highly competent surgeon still, Sandy Drummond was a wreck of the man he had once been. Square and big-boned, he was bald and overweight, while his eyes looked out from between folds of discolored flesh. But today he was a much fitter man than Michael Adversane, and they both knew it.

'It's still infected,' Michael said flatly. 'And the blood supply, as you say, hopelessly reduced. Hardly surprising, of course.'

'What I want to do is take you into the theater again to explore the main vessels in the damaged area. See if there's anything we can do to improve matters.' He shook his head. 'I must admit, I'm not very hopeful about it,' he said. 'Now, Mike, I'm afraid we have to face it. If we're unsuccessful, if we fail in our efforts to improve the circulation – and I'm not optimistic, as I've said – then either you're going to need another operation again later, or you can leave us to make the decision for you, and act, if in our opinion there's nothing more to be done.' His gentle brown eyes held compassion, as Michael had seen them so often before when he had placed an unwelcome but inexorable decision squarely before a patient. They both knew what he meant now, and Michael looked broodingly back at him, for the first time in his career not envying him his job.

'I knew this was coming,' he said. 'I've known it for days, I think. You go ahead. Do whatever you have to do.' He set his lips.

'Tomorrow morning, then,' Sandy said abruptly. 'At the beginning of my list.'

Michael was shaken. 'As soon as that?' he asked, a tremor discernible in the voice he intended to sound steady, unemotional.

'No point in hanging about.' The longer Michael had to think over the possibilities ahead, the less he'd care for them, Sandy knew. 'Northiam's free then,' he added, to clinch it.

Marcus Northiam was the Central's heart surgeon. His fame was international, his advice the best in Europe. But once he'd been called in, his opinion would have to be accepted. 'Right,' Michael agreed curtly. 'Go ahead.'

Later the same evening Sandy looked in again. 'How are you feeling, Mike?'

He shrugged. 'Robbie brought me a consent form. I've signed it. The rest is up to you.' He was angrily aware that a tremor hovered once again in his voice. The less he said the better.

'I've warned your grandmother,' Sandy told him.

'I know. She's been in.'

'She says she intends to be present in the

23

theater,' Sandy was uneasy about this.

'Yes. She's set on it. I think it's a mistake.'

'So do I. No good trying to stop her when she's made up her mind, though. Is she coming in to see you tonight?'

'No. At least I talked her out of that.' Lady Adversane, vigorous still and immersed in laboratory techniques and the training of students, was in her eighties now, and tired quickly, though she would rarely admit this. 'I pointed out that if she was determined to be up and in the theater first thing tomorrow morning, she'd better go home and have a quiet evening and an early night.'

'And the same goes for you, Mike,' Sandy said firmly.

Michael nodded. 'I'll let them settle me down as early as they like,' he promised.

But it was a promise he found it impossible to keep. He was understandably unwilling, when the moment came, to take the two tablets that would allow the day to close. Tomorrow would bring a challenge he suspected he was unprepared to meet. He had sent Robbie Pollock, Sandy's house surgeon, away, the night staff nurse too, and his light was still on when a head came around the door. Julian Northcott, one of his oldest friends, and a registrar on the General Surgical Unit.

'Hello, come in.'

'I thought you might be asleep.'

24

'I'm not in any hurry, frankly.'

'No, I suppose not.'

Julian, Michael saw at once, was trying to conceal what he obviously considered to be inappropriate elation. Michael guessed the cause immediately. Julian had been out with Rachel. He decided to make it easy for him. Julian would never get around to opening the subject otherwise, but he'd every right, after all, to take Rachel out. There was nothing to be gained by making a heavy secret of it. He and Julian had known one another too long to allow awkward silences to develop at this juncture. 'How's Rachel?' he asked. At least to talk about her would be a change from dwelling on the possible findings in the theater tomorrow.

Julian, however, thought otherwise. 'Oh – er – fine. Fine. We – er – we had a bit of supper together, you know, and I – I told her about your operation tomorrow.' He was eaten alive with guilt, 'I explained–'

'So what did she say?'

Julian went over to the window and fiddled with the blind, his back turned. 'She – she sent you her best wishes,' he said inadequately. He had in fact suggested that Rachel should come with him and deliver these wishes in person, but she hadn't felt up to it.

Michael grunted. To have seen Rachel tonight would have raised his spirits, he knew, lifted him out of the despondency that had engulfed him. On the other hand, perhaps it was as well she had not come. With her blonde fragility, her wide doe-eyed timidity, she had appealed above all to his protective instincts. Now he was in no position to protect anyone. Better to leave Julian to look after her.

He was miserable about the whole affair. He shifted his feet. 'Hell, I'm sorry, Mike.'

'Me too. But there it is. Nothing to be done.' Nothing to be done about anything. Either Rachel, or his damaged leg.

Julian turned around at last, and they stared at one another without pretense. They had been friends since they were students, had shared hopes and fears, success and failure. Until now, more success than failure. Both of them were clever, able, highly competent, though their friendship had been largely an attraction of opposites. Michael was sociable, pleasure-loving, active, gregarious. Julian, by contrast, was a quiet introverted intellectual, with fewer friendships but those few long-standing. Tonight he was thoroughly unhappy. He was too honest and too bad an actor to provide cheerful reassurance in this situation. He could think of nothing encouraging to say, and finally he mumbled a few platitudes, muttered something about his round, and left.

Michael picked up the evening paper, read

it with concentrated determination.

His next visitor was Leo Rosenstein. Because of Michael's illness, he had agreed to stay on as Resident Surgical Officer for an additional six months. 'You all right?' he inquired.

'Yes, thanks.'

These two were old enemies. Leo, three years senior to Michael, behaved still, after fifteen years at the Central, as if he had strayed in from the barrow at the gates. His voice was straight unadulterated cockney – according to some, increasingly cockney with every step he took up the ladder of pro-motion. He was, everyone could see, going to climb right to the top. He had no under-standing of this himself, though occasionally he was a little puzzled by the slowness and ineptitude of most of his colleagues. Michael Adversane though, had always been a double threat. Self-assured, endowed by birth with all the worldly advantages Leo himself so conspicuously lacked, Michael had the knack of arousing in Leo an uncomfortable awareness of all the deficiencies he needed to put behind him. The wrong voice, the wrong clothes, the wrong school, the wrong family. As Michael had followed Leo up the medical school and then the hospital hierarchy, three years behind always, it was in his presence that Leo found himself ashamed of his origins, saw himself as an insecure interloper, soon to be overtaken and passed by young Adversane, who really belonged. When Michael was a newly qualified house surgeon, Leo had been his registrar, and he had used every opportunity he could seize – and they were not few – to demonstrate his junior's ignorance and incompetence. Michael had stood up to it without flinching or panicking, and as the years went by their antagonism and constant sparring became an accepted entertainment on the surgical side.

Leo was corpulent already, a head shorter than Michael, but strong, virile, ebullient. A kind man, normally, and an outstanding surgeon. And, of course, observant.

'What are those doin' there?' he demanded immediately, pointing with his strong neat little finger at the two tablets on the side table. Leo had surprisingly small hands.

'I'll take them later.' Mike hardly looked up from the paper.

Leo retreated to the end of the bed, began reading the notes. 'Robbie's bin over you, I see.'

'Yep.'

'So if 'e's bin over you, why didn't 'e settle you dahn? Eh?'

'Because I told him not to. I'll settle myself down.'

'Julian bin in?'

'Yep.'

Leo was surprised. "E 'as? Then why didn't 'e see you took your tablets? And turn your flippin' light orf, seein' as 'ow you're too – obstinate to do it for yourself?'

'He had other things on his mind.'

'Other fings on 'is – mind? Cor stone the crows. Well, I 'aven't, see? 'Ere you are, stop playing about and swallow 'em.' He handed over the tablets and a glass of water. His voice was thick and dominating – it would have dominated the population of a sixteen-story block in the Mile End Road – but his eyes for once were gentle. 'You can't 'old back the dawn, mate, so give over tryin', eh?'

Michael's smile flickered briefly. 'You are so right.' He swallowed the tablets. 'Roll on tomorrow.'

Leo touched him lightly on the shoulder. In all the years they had worked together, he had never deliberately touched Michael before. 'Night,' he said. He turned off the bedside light, scooped up the crumpled pages of the evening papers, announcing, 'I'll take these, you won't be needing them,' and was gone. Outside the door he conferred with the staff nurse, who came quietly in and straightened everything that could be straightened. Then Michael was alone, with five or ten minutes before the drug worked in which to contemplate the morning and its implications.

The time was snatched from him. A head came cautiously around the door. 'Mike?' it breathed. Jane.

'Come in,' he said, his voice surprised. He had not expected to see her.

She sat down beside him, a tall well-made girl in shabby jeans, with the wide Drummond mouth and the well-covered Drummond frame. A mass of red hair, and Sandy's soft brown eyes. 'I just wanted to – to wish you luck.'

'I'll need it.'

'Oh, Mike, it's hell for you.' She took his hand and held it tightly. Jane Drummond had been holding Michael Adversane's hand tightly from the age of eighteen months, when she had staggered about the lawn supported by a serious seven-year-old. This was the first occasion on which he had found her grip reassuring. Until now, the demands had been on her side.

'I've taken my drugs,' he warned her.

'Oh, Mike, I'm disturbing you. Anyway, they'll kill me if they find me here. Sleep well.' She put her hand against his temple, dropped a fleeting kiss in the same place, then drew the sheet around him as though he had been in the nursery.

Her touch was to remain his last memory of that night carrying him easily into unperturbed sleep. The drug put him out completely, and in the early morning, while he was faintly aware of the commotion that went on, he found it easy to sink back into a waking doze and ignore the bustle. No one brought him tea, and the first real moment of consciousness he knew was when Robbie materialized, muttering about pre-med. He was worried and overanxious, jumpily on edge, to reassure him seemed only natural, and then the pre-medication began to act and detachment set in.

In the anesthetic room his grandmother appeared fleetingly, curiously lost, uncertain – most unlike her. Again he felt he ought to provide support and encouragement, but could see no logical means of doing so. Had he only known it, she was possessed by similar emotions. Fortunately the Director of the Biochemistry Laboratory, a former student of hers, was escorting her – she never lacked an entourage – and as soon as Michael's eye caught his, took her arm and led her on into the theater.

This was crowded. Sandy Drummond was to be assisted by Leo, already there with his registrar, in addition to Robbie Pollock, shaking visibly. Just as well, Leo thought, that Robbie would not be called on for much in the way of performance. Lord Mummery, with his registrar, was standing by to support Sandy Drummond if the necessity came – as they all knew it might – to make a difficult decision. Marcus Northiam, the heart surgeon – small, spare, graying – came in, with his chief assistant, James Leyburn.

Michael was wheeled in, accompanied by the consultant anesthetist, director of the Central's Intensive Care Unit.

Sandy looked across the table. 'We've been into this before, I know,' he said. 'Just a last check. We have plenty of blood? We may need it.'

The words dropped coldly.

'We have six bottles,' Sister Hill said.

'And we have six more waiting in the unit,' the anesthetist added.

Soon all that could be seen of Michael Adversane was the site of operation, his scarred and infected leg. Sandy made the first incision, began a muttered colloquy with Northiam and Leo Rosenstein. He began to dissect out the branches of the main blood vessels behind the knee.

They looked pessimistically at the result. 'Any chance at all, do you think, Marcus, of repair here that could result in an adequate blood supply?' Sandy asked finally. He hardly needed Northiam to provide an answer. He could see for himself.

Northiam regarded the narrow strings that had once been great pulsing arteries. 'No technique we have at present can remedy this sort of condition,' he said shortly. 'Too much damage. Too big a gap to be bridged.'

'You don't think,' Sandy began, 'if perhaps

we were able to...' He put forward a suggestion he knew very well was unworkable. But they had to consider every possibility of saving the limb, thrash out the arguments for and against, explore all contingencies. They discussed it up and down, but there was, as Northiam said, no remedy. They knew it.

'There's the infection too,' Mummery said. 'With all that dead tissue, it's easy to see why the antibiotics are ineffective. They can't reach the seat of the trouble at all.'

'Quite so,' Northiam agreed. 'I think we must assume the bloodstream is being reinfected from this limb. You'll have to remove it.' Typically, he spoke out while the rest of them hesitated still. 'Take the leg off. He's not going to mend until you do. Once the leg's gone, the antibiotics will have a chance. You ought to be able to extinguish the remainder of the infection without too much difficulty then. Or that's my opinion.'

Sandy's head was bent, for a moment he did not raise it, while his hands were still. He looked up, across to Lord Mummery. Their eyes met. 'I'm afraid we have no option,' Sandy said.

'None at all.' Mummery was decisive. 'I agree with Northiam.'

'Lady Adversane, we shall have to go on and amputate,' Sandy said, his voice slow and deliberate.

'It is essential,' she agreed, in her usual clear and bell-like tones. 'I'm sure Mr Northiam is quite correct.'

The men looked at her a little helplessly.

There was a brief silence. No one moved. Finally Sandy stared hard and meaningfully at the Director of the Biochemistry Laboratory, who belatedly understood his own function, stepped into the breach. 'I think, Lady Adversane, that the surgeons can dispense with our presence now,' he said in his pedantic way. 'No further purpose can be served by – m-mm – ah – m-mm – by … only distress yourself unnecessarily … m-mm–' his voice wavered and died away. Was she going to be difficult? How long was it since she had watched a major operation? An amputation was a procedure even the surgeons and theater staff dreaded. You could almost feel the heavy silence that had descended on the small group around the table under the blinding light. Inspiration visited him, or so he mistakenly imagined. 'Extremely hot in here,' he added. 'Very fatiguing.'

It was an error. She looked him up and down disparagingly. 'Out of condition. Overweight,' she reported, with her usual clarity and precision. A great deal of nervous tension was released in the quiver that swept through the theater at this accurate description of one of the leading biochemists in the country. Lady Adversane herself was sublimely aware that she had spoken her thoughts aloud, and continued briskly: 'You are quite right. We should go now, as you say.' She imagined this to be her only reply. 'Thank you, Sir Alexander. I know you will do everything that can be done.' She turned and went out, accompanied by a chastened biochemist.

Sister Hill nodded at her staff nurse, and the amputation trolley was wheeled into position.

2

Rachel

Times had changed for the Adversanes, Sandy thought sadly. The house in Harley Street was quiet and empty these days. Old Freddie had died two years ago, and there were only two Adversanes left, Michael and his grandmother. When Sandy had been a medical student with Michael's father James, the Adversanes had struck him as grand, important, bathed in an almost tangible glow of worldly success. To the young Sandy, who knew no one in London and had no influence anywhere, the house in Harley Street had glittered, had seemed to be the hub of the universe.

He and James had qualified, had gone up the hospital together – James like his father in medicine, Sandy in surgery. They had both married. Surprisingly, it was James who made the sensible marriage, to Clare Monteith, the senior staff nurse in outpatients, a pleasant level-headed girl with steady eyes and no affectations. Sandy had married his lovely Elspeth, and lived to regret it.

The war had come, and eventually both

James and Sandy found themselves in the R.A.M.C. in North Africa, where James was killed. Clare, with their baby son, lived with the Adversanes in Harley Street. Then she too had been killed – ironically enough, not in London at all, but by a V-bomb when she had gone to the Kentish countryside for a weekend's walking with another sister from the Central, leaving two-year-old Michael in the care of his grandparents.

He had been brought up by his grandparents – and by Sandy, his godfather. Since the final breakdown of his marriage and the departure of Elspeth to the USA, the two human beings who mattered above all to Sandy had been Jane and Michael. In his secret mind he had often planned their marriage. Now his hopes were centred on Michael's mere survival.

He sat beside Michael's bed now in the Intensive Care Unit, glancing at the monitor recording his heartbeat, automatically checking the drip that was replenishing his blood supply, noting without knowing that he did so the functioning of the drainage tubes.

Regardless of the monitor, Sandy had his finger on Michael's wrist, taking his pulse. At any minute he would come around. Sandy would be there when he did so.

Michael's eyes opened. Vague and trusting, they sought Sandy's and apparently found satisfaction. They closed again and he slept. Sandy's own forehead was wet with perspiration. It had been hot, of course, in the theater all morning, and it was always very warm in the Intensive Care Unit. But this hardly accounted for the beads of sweat at which he was dabbing now with his handkerchief. The dreaded encounter had come and gone, with no demands.

Breaking the news could be postponed, might even be left to others. To sister, perhaps, or to Robbie Pollock. Or Lady Adversane, who was, after all, his next of kin, and medically qualified. Was Sandy himself to spend the remainder of his own overfull day here, appointments cancelled left and right?

He was to do exactly this, though in fact it was a matter of half an hour only before Michael reopened his eyes vaguely again, but with a glimmer of wondering puzzlement rising to the surface. Again he looked for Sandy, but this time without trust. With wary appraisal. 'Well?' he inquired, finding his voice not strong and challenging, as he had assumed it would be, but a husky whisper. He frowned, irritated and suspicious.

Sandy kept one finger on his pulse – a pulse that was behaving oddly – and his other hand grasped Michael's securely.

'Tell me,' the husky voice insisted.

Sandy did so, step by step, no omissions. When he came to the end, Michael lay still and silent, his eyes closed, his face no paler than it had been earlier. Only the monitor broadcast his reaction to all who cared to read it, and the grip he kept on Sandy's hand told Sandy more.

Sister Paré looked in, questioned Sandy by a quick lift of one eyebrow. He answered her with a slight nod. Pain momentarily shadowed the plain face under its frilly cap, then she was gone, back to her busy ward.

Leo came in, stood there swaying back and forward, his eyes veering from the monitor to Michael to Sandy. They communicated without words – Leo was good at this – and Leo nodded. 'I'll do yer round, sir,' he said, and was gone.

Later still Jane came in. Her father glanced up, smiled in welcome, though his face remained heavy with sorrow. She came across to him, looked at Michael. He was lying with his eyes closed, apparently sleeping.

'Have you…'

Sandy nodded. 'I told him.'

'Oh.' Jane leaned against her father, her bones suddenly turned to water as the long agony of that morning in the gallery of the orthopedic theater took its toll. Sandy put his arm around her.

In the residents' mess, Michael Adversane's admission to his own ward and the surgery he had undergone were to remain a major topic. They assessed his chances constantly, discussed his reactions. Of course, no one expected him to accept the disaster that had overtaken him in a matter of days. But they were surprised how hard he fought against it.

'He's not adjusting at all,' they told one another.

'Well, would you?'

'Man is an adaptable animal.'

'Not the Adversanes. Life adjusts to them. They're programmed for success only.'

'You're right. Mike has no experience of defeat. He's had no previous setbacks to teach him. Nothing to fall back on.'

Michael would have agreed. This was how he felt. Out of the blue, with no warning, life had been snatched from under him, and he had nothing to fall back on. In theory he ought to have known exactly what he had to face. But the reality was different. Conflicting emotions possessed him. One moment he wanted nothing more than to turn the clock back, to be fit and well and working in the theater. Then suddenly grief for his lost limb swept him, and all the cells of his body seemed to be crying out in bereavement. Distress consumed him, like the uncontrollable tears of a child, when least expected. He fought the distress, as he fought it all. He could not – would not – accept himself as an invalid. Or as a cripple. He had been active always, a surgeon and a mountaineer. His eyes turned back again to the lost past, renewed the useless struggle to regain it – and himself as he had been.

At first they kept him under sedation. People he knew came and went around him in a muddled fashion, melting into one another as though in a dream. He'd think it was Sandy he was talking to, but then he'd discover it was no longer Sandy but Leo. Or Leo would merge into Jane. She came regularly to see him, ostensibly looking for her father in the ward, and just taking the opportunity of dropping in on Michael. She deceived him, but not Sister Paré's acute eye.

Inevitably the clear spells took over, and the days at last assumed a pattern of morning, afternoon and evening. His regular visitors began to make their own pattern. Sandy and Leo three times a day, of course, Lady Adversane in the afternoon, Jane usually in the evening. Until he found himself lying all day long in the small room off Ambroise Paré ward, he had never noticed that footsteps were almost as distinctive as voices. Now, though, he lay in bed, and knew instantly who was in the corridor. The sound of Sandy approaching with Robbie, or of Leo on his way. He knew his grandmother's quick staccato patter, and Jane's light step was immediately recognizable. Each of the nurses, and Sister Paré, soon had her own rhythm. He began to make forecasts, and found himself absurdly disappointed if he was mistaken, or if the footsteps he had recognized went on past his door, en route for another part of the hospital. His eyes flew to the door of his room so frequently that even Lady Adversane noticed.

'Are you expecting someone, Michael?'

'No,' he said sharply. Who was it he expected? He hardly knew himself.

'I saw your friend Julian Northcott as I came across from the other block,' she announced one afternoon. 'He didn't see me, though. Lost in a dream, I suppose. A very *vague* young man.' Her most damning criticism.

Michael defended Julian automatically. 'Not vague. Only concentrated. Then he never sees anyone.' In fact, though, he had received a nasty jolt.

So Julian was around the place.

Then why hadn't he been in to see him? Michael sought around in his mind, came up with no answer. Until now, he had been assuming that the reason he had not seen Julian must be that the thoracic theater was unexpectedly slack, and he had been able to take some overdue leave. But he was there in the hospital, and he could hardly be so busy that he'd had no opportunity even to stick his head around the door. When he'd told Julian to look after Rachel, the last thing he'd imagined was that they'd both disappear out of his life. Julian and he had known each other for over ten years. How could he suddenly vanish like this?

Julian's difficulty was simple. He had no idea what to say to Michael. Rachel absorbed him, he was lost in a new and precarious happiness, and he was afraid Michael would instantly discover this if they met. He had not the heart to explain to Michael, at this point in his illness, that he had been unable to prevent himself from falling hopelessly in love with Rachel. The surprise had been that there turned out to be nothing hopeless about it. Rachel's fragile timidity had always made as strong an appeal to him as it had done to Michael, and he had loved her from the moment they met. He had been over-shadowed then, as so often before, by Michael – tall, charming, dominating, with an air of unconscious authority, and the Adversane aura of success. But now Michael was out of the running, Julian had his chance at last. Unhesitatingly he took it. Love for Rachel possessed him, and all other considerations paled. Guilt invaded him too – so he avoided the side room on Ambroise Paré.

The hospital watched, of course. And condemned.

'How can he be so heartless? Michael was

supposed to be his friend, after all. I would never have believed Julian could behave like this.'

'He's a surgeon, too. He ought to know what this might do to Michael. He'd know all right if it was one of his patients. He'd be the first to say any patient of his was entitled to all the postoperative support he could get.' The sisters were arguing it out over coffee.

'Anyway, whatever Julian does, you'd think Rachel at least would be thinking of Michael. You'd expect her to want to help him through. She ought not to have any time for Julian.'

'Such a soft slip of a girl,' one of the older sisters commented. 'I thought she'd be loving and devoted.'

'She's loving and devoted all right. But to Julian. She's simply switched blokes. Mike's no good to her now, but luckily Julian's right there in the queue.' Barbie Henderson, Sister General Theater, was bitter. She had been a staff nurse on the orthopedic theater when Michael Adversane had been a house surgeon. She had loved him then, and she loved him still. She knew she could never have walked out on him.

But Rachel was looking for security. As Michael had always known, she was vulnerable. Life itself frightened her. Michael's illness appalled her. In any case, she had always been wary of him, uneasy. He was too popular, in too much demand. She had never dared to count on him. Surgery, mountain-eering expeditions, the fact that since his grandfather's death he had had to escort Lady Adversane – all this left him limited time for his personal life. Though she had never admitted it to herself, this had suited Rachel. To be taken about at all by Michael was like a drive in a fast car. Exhilarating, but terrifying. A little went a long way, and small doses of Michael Adversane had always been more than enough for Rachel. Sometimes she had tried to imagine herself married to him. An exciting prospect, but the details blurred, and secretly she knew that the reality would have overwhelmed her. She could never have stood the pace. Marrying Julian, though, was entirely different. It would be everything she was looking for. Above all he would be reliable. He was gentle and kind, and he would be in her life forever.

She too was guilty, of course, about Michael. 'Ought I to go and see him?' she asked Julian uneasily.

'I'm sure he'd like it if you did.' Julian was always honest – one of his difficulties.

'But what on earth could I say to him?' Rachel asked blankly.

This was Julian's problem too.

Neither of them was able to deal with it. As the days went by, they avoided Michael, but grew to know one another well. Soon they were deeply in love. They could hardly remember anyone else existed.

In the ward, Michael lay inert, too weak as yet to learn to move about on the temporary prosthesis that waited with a walking frame in the corner of the room, too depressed and despondent to fight against the lassitude that crept insidiously over him. As the weeks went by, he failed to rally, instead grew increasingly listless, remote, unresponsive. They were giving him a stiff course of antibiotics to combat the infection, but the fever had not yet left him, and vitality drained out of him daily.

In the surgical block they were worried. 'The infection still has a hold on him,' Sandy told Lord Mummery. 'I'm afraid he's deteriorating. Of course, he was pretty well exhausted by the time we got him back here at last, and he's had major surgery since. I hope he'll begin to pick up soon. But at present I must say I don't care for the look of him.'

'Let's hope he hasn't acquired some nasty bug in those Nepalese villages that we aren't going to be able to eliminate,' Lord Mummery said depressingly. 'I'll go in and have a look at him myself, shall I?'

'I'd be grateful if you would,' Sandy said.

The next morning Lord Mummery finished his ward round, and was on his way out when he recollected this conversation. He swung on his heel, turned off unexpectedly along the corridor and into Michael's room. His startled entourage had wheeled with him, and soon filled the small room, overflowing into the corridor, peering over shoulders – Leo, Lord Mummery's registrar and house surgeon, two visiting Americans, several Indians, an Australian and a Nigerian, with Sister Paré, a medical social worker, a physiotherapist and the students, among them Jane Drummond, her finals only a month or two away. At least twenty people halted respectfully while Lord Mummery carried on a one-sided conversation with a monosyllabic Michael Adversane. The students had last encountered him as the busy active senior registrar, who taught them, occasionally intimidated them, always impressed them. Now he had collapsed into this slight crumpled figure, unshaven, pale to the point of transparency. His replies to Lord Mummery were inaudible. All he wanted was to be left alone.

Eventually, of course, he was. Lord Mummery, followed by Leo and the rest of them, departed.

The effects of this encounter on the students was electric. The medical school could talk of nothing else.

Jane was furious. 'You'd be laid out if you'd been through half of what he's had to face,' she asserted, sparks flying from her normally gentle eyes, off her red hair. 'It doesn't mean he won't pull out of it.'

Talking about Lord Mummery's opinion of Michael's condition at lunch in the residents' mess, Leo discovered for the first time that Julian had not seen him. At the table everyone stopped eating. Heads turned abruptly. No one spoke at first. Most of them on the surgical side had looked in on him on their rounds, many from the medical side had gone over to Ambroise Paré especially, pathologists, physiologists, radiologists – they'd all been in to visit Michael. None of them had been as close a friend as Julian. At first they didn't believe what he told them. They thought he must simply mean he hadn't been in that particular day.

'No,' Julian maintained, harassed but truthful. 'I haven't seen him at all. Actually. No.'

A chorus of inquiry broke out. Leo quelled it. 'Go in now.'

Julian looked at his watch. 'I've a clinic at two.'

'Only 1:45. You don't need coffee. Go now.'

'Well, I–'

'Stone the crows. 'Ave I got to drag you there?'

'No, of course not, Leo. It's just that I–'

'Start walkin', mate.'

49

Julian started.

'I've noticed it before,' the Resident Medical Officer commented. 'Julian always needs telling what to do. Good brain, not much initiative or independence. Mike used to run him, you know. He wasn't aware he did, I'm sure.'

'I ought to 'ave spotted it,' Leo said, annoyed with himself. 'Never crossed what passes for me mind that 'e hadn't so much as bin in to see the bloke.'

'I hope he gets there now,' the R.M.O. suggested. 'It wouldn't take much to divert him, I don't suppose.'

''E'll get there,' Leo said ominously. He left the room himself, jet-propelled.

They looked at each other. 'Who'd have believed it? Leo battling away in support of Adversane?'

'Who'd believe any of it?' the senior surgical registrar asked. 'Either that disaster would hit Mike Adversane, of all people, or that when it did, his closest friend would choose that moment simply to walk off with Mike's dreamy blonde?'

'It's outrageous of Julian. I thought he was a quiet kindly individual.'

'We all know why he's chosen this particular moment to do it. He didn't have a chance before.'

'Unforgivable. That's why he hasn't been to see Mike, of course. Ashamed.'

50

'Daren't face him.'

'No wonder poor old Mike's in a bad way. This could easily finish him off, if you ask me.'

'It's the sort of thing that does finish people off, I agree,' the R.M.O. said slowly. 'But, you know, I don't think it will in this case. Mike has more stamina than that. But he's up against it, no doubt of that.'

He was, and in a way they did not foresee.

When Julian – pushed almost physically, and certainly morally, through the door by Leo – appeared in his room, Mike's first words were, 'Hello, there you are. I was wondering where you'd got to.'

Julian flushed, and mumbled something about being rather busy.

'How's Rachel?'

An entirely natural inquiry, it was over-heard by Leo, standing in the doorway blocking Julian's escape route. That evening he pinned Julian down in a corridor, told him to send Rachel to visit Michael the following day.

Julian hedged and dithered, but finally gave in. He was no match for Leo. Rachel in her turn tried to evade the summons. Julian, though, was in awe of Leo. He knew he could not face him the next morning unless Rachel had paid the promised visit. His own guilty conscience pushed him into action, too. He remained, for once, adamant, and it

51

was Rachel who had to give in.

To brace them both, Julian took her out for an expensive meal in Soho. Candlelight, a small table for two, a crisp white cloth, and across the table, in the soft light, Rachel's huge speaking eyes. Julian spent lavishly. Double gins, scampi, a stupendous coq au vin, and a dessert of fresh pineapple whipped up with cream and liqueur. A bottle of cold wine from the Loire, then strong black coffee and brandy to set the seal on their resolution.

Only it failed to achieve this. Rachel remained terrified. 'What on earth can I *say* to him?' she demanded again and again. 'I shan't know what to say. I'm desperately sorry for him, but I can't tell him that. You don't understand, Julian. I'm no good when people are ill. Illness does something to me. I can't help it, I simply go to pieces.'

And this was precisely what she did, when Julian ushered her into Michael's room, rather later than he had planned, as their meal had been a prolonged affair. Michael was expecting no one other than the staff on their rounds, but he was genuinely pleased to see Julian and Rachel.

However she might inwardly feel, Rachel was looking her loveliest. She had dressed carefully for her meal with Julian, and her pale fragility was afloat in swirling pastel chiffon, ankle length, the latest full bishop sleeves emphasizing her frail bird-boned wrists and long-fingered eloquent hands. Above the soft collar her peaky face, eyes wider than ever with panic, glimmered mistily, as though in a dream – a nostalgic dream of the past for Michael. He pulled himself abruptly together, relieved to find he possessed the ability. He must play this very cool indeed. 'Hi,' he said huskily. 'It's you two. Great to see you both.'

Rachel did not find it in any way great to see him. She gulped. Julian had tried to explain to her that she would find Michael changed, but even so, she was unprepared for the physical deterioration confronting her now. She gulped again, took another look at him, and broke down. Julian had to remove her hastily, weeping bitterly and uncontrollably.

The shock to Michael was profound. Never before in his thirty years had any girl dissolved into tears at the mere sight of him. He stared, numb with sheer astonishment at first, at the opposite wall. He had foreseen a great deal, but he had never expected anything like this.

He lay where he was. After all, he had no alternative.

When the staff nurse came in half an hour later, she took one look at his color, which was ashen, and his closed eyes. She felt for his pulse, pressed the bell for assistance, raised his lids. The student nurse who was on with her that night came at the gallop. 'Ring the cardiac emergency bell, and come back here with the resuscitation bag,' the other girl told her briefly.

Jane, on her way to the thoracic theater to check on the next morning's list, flattened herself against the wall as the resuscitation team thundered past with their trolley. She continued on her way to the office, and asked casually as she entered, 'Cardiac emergency?'

'Apparently, on Ambroise Paré,' the nurse at the desk told her absently, her finger marking the entry she was transferring across.

Jane's color ebbed. 'Paré? You don't know who, I suppose?'

The nurse was writing again. 'No, sorry,' she said without looking up. A daft question, she considered. But then the students were daft.

Jane told herself not to be silly. There were sixty patients on Ambroise Paré. Just the same, she turned around, fled downstairs and across to the orthopedic block. As soon as she reached Paré she went along the corridor to Michael's door. It was wide open, the small room bursting with white coats, and the bed pulled out from the wall.

3

A Clinic in Switzerland

Jane could not see Michael at all. They had him almost standing on his head, his face covered by an oxygen mask.

There was sudden movement behind her as Leo shouldered his way through the throng. 'What's goin' on 'ere?' he demanded. 'Stone the crows. When did this 'appen?' Several voices enlightened him. They were in the process of taking an electrocardiogram, and all eyes were watching the flickering needle.

Leo spared a quick glance for Jane. 'Don't know what you think you're doin' 'ere,' he commented unappreciatively. He thought her color almost as bad as the patient's. 'Still, as you are around, you can go out and look for Lady Adversane. I passed 'er on me way. You'd better meet 'er and 'old 'er 'and. I'll let you know if there's any change.'

Jane did as he said. Most people obeyed Leo. She went out into the corridor and saw Lady Adversane's erect, indomitable figure approaching at its usual rapid trot. Leo must have shown a considerable turn of speed, she understood with immediately increased anxiety, to have passed her at all. She went to meet her. 'He's having oxygen,' she said, her voice striving for normality, for calm reassurance. 'Leo Rosenstein's in there with him. He asked me to wait here with you.'

The blue eyes so amazingly like Michael's swept over her, saw more than Jane bargained for. 'Thank you, my dear. We'll stay here together, shall we?' It was a moot point who was reassuring whom.

A student nurse appeared with two chairs, and they sat in the corridor together for what seemed to both of them several hours. In fact it was thirty minutes or so before Leo's bulky form appeared. Genuine reassurance was at once evident, quite distinct from the phoney version they had been offering one another.

'Storm in a teacup,' he said unemotionally. 'Not an embolus, or a coronary. You can relax. No more than a faint, and a drop in blood pressure. Probably 'e 'ad a stiff bout of pain, somethin' like that. You can come in and 'ave a look, if you like.' His voice dared them to do anything of the sort. 'But 'e's dropping off to sleep comfortably.'

As soon as she could, immediately the course of treatment ended, Lady Adversane took a hand and whisked Michael off to Switzerland to convalesce. Jane was furious, disapproved strongly of the plan, but no one listened to her. He was unfit even to sit up in a chair, and had to be transported as a stretcher case by prior arrangement with B.E.A. Lady Adversane went with him, accompanied by her old friend Dr Sybil Ormerod, recently retired from general practice in Kensington, and Sister Wood, a Central-trained nurse now in her sixties, who had always looked after Freddie Adversane's private cases. Michael looked at the three of them with ingratitude and deep loathing. His own entourage – three old ladies. This was what it had come to.

He and Sister Wood were deposited in an expensive clinic, while Lady Adversane and Dr Ormerod stayed at a nearby – and equally expensive – hotel. They spent their days pottering about collecting alpine flowers and drinking coffee. Michael spent his in bed on his balcony, ministered to with kindness and unalterable patience by Sister Wood.

The snowcapped peaks maddened him. Only a few months ago he could have been climbing up through the meadows resonant with cowbells, up past the chalets where villagers looked after the cattle pastured for the summer on the high slopes, up above the snow line to attempt a difficult ascent by the as yet unconquered route. Now his grandmother and Dr Ormerod, in their eighties, were disporting themselves on the slopes while he lay immobilized on this damned balcony.

For years now he had spent all his free time in the mountains, and his life could almost be measured in the peaks he had climbed. This part of Switzerland, as it happened, represented the nursery slopes. Here he had come with parties from school led by Rupert Fiske. Here, too, he had introduced Jane to the mountains. He had been a medical student then, Jane still at school. They had gone in a group of ten. Michael the leader, traveling the cheap way, boat from Newhaven to Dieppe, then across France and into Switzerland by rail, second class, rattling and banging through the night, decanted in a gray dawn at Basle, exhausted, sleepy-eyed, with rucksack, rolled sleeping bag, hung around with ice axe, best nylon rope, crampons, pitons, climbing boots.

He remembered their first breakfast at Basle station, waiting for their connection. Gallons of wonderful Swiss coffee, fresh rolls and butter, black cherry jam. Jane, stupefied with sleep, stumbling so that he had put his arm out to hold her up. He would never be able to do that again.

No more climbing for him. No more expeditions with Jane. She'd been like a younger sister all his life. Admiring, ready to share any experience, to follow loyally where he led. Ready, too, to seek his advice in any problem, at school or at home – where she had her difficulties, after all, for Jane was the child of a broken marriage. Only sixteen, she had made the hard decision, fought bitterly by her mother, to stay with her father when Elspeth Drummond had eventually left for the States on her remarriage. Michael had seen her through that crisis. Today, with his own life in fragments, he would have liked to turn to her. But she had her finals coming up in less than a month, as he well knew. After all, he'd been one of her teachers. She must not have her concentration disturbed. He wouldn't even write to her – she'd have to take precious reviewing time to answer him.

Soon Jane would be qualified, walking the wards at the Central as a house surgeon, as her father had done before her. But Michael would not be there to see her. She too would go on without him, as Julian and Rachel had gone, as life went on regardless. The gap he had left quickly closed. He had seen it happen to others. He had never expected it to happen to him.

Here in Switzerland he began at last to face the fact that the past was behind him. The future would be different. But he could not begin to accept it. There would be no more climbing. Very likely there would be no more surgery. Certainly he would never be R.S.O. at the Central, taking Leo's place.

What was he to do with his life? All that he cared about had been snatched from him during those few unlucky moments on a Himalayan mountainside. If only he'd been a yard or two further to his left when the avalanche had crashed down, he'd have his leg today – and the R.S.O's post. In honesty, he had to admit that a yard or two further to the right, and he would not be alive now to do any worrying about his career. This thought, however, failed to raise his spirits noticeably.

Lady Adversane remained unaware at first of the depression that was demoralizing him more surely here in the Swiss clinic than it had ever done in his room on Ambroise Paré. On the contrary, she considered there had been a problem, which she had dealt with admirably. Michael had always loved the mountains. He would enjoy it here. As soon as he was stronger, Sister Wood could wheel him among the alpine meadows in their spring glory.

Michael was damned if he'd be wheeled anywhere. Sister Wood found him unco-operative, and the fact gave her sleepless nights. After all her years of experience – and with difficult patients, too. In her time she'd nursed them all. Self-willed tycoons, spoiled young wives, temperamental actresses, vola-tile writers, ebullient film directors, members of parliament worried about their public image, country wives worried about the dog's exercise. You name them. Sister Wood had nursed them while they were under the high-powered care of Sir Frederick Adversane. But Michael Adversane was too much for her. Of course, doctors always made the worst patients. Even so, she ought to be able to manage him. Lady Adversane would think she was too old, past it.

In fact, though, Lady Adversane apologized. 'I'm afraid my grandson is giving you a difficult time, Sister.'

'Oh no, of course not, Lady Adversane,' Sister Wood protested sycophantically, immediately giving the lie to this statement by adding, 'poor boy, he can't help it. It's not to be wondered at.'

Lady Adversane and Dr Ormerod looked at one another. Their suspicions were confirmed. While they explored the flowery slopes, Michael was giving poor Sister Wood hell.

'He's not getting on as I would like,' Dr Ormerod admitted. 'He ought to be getting about a bit by now.'

Sister Wood tutted. 'Poor boy, he has had a bad time. It's not surprising he's a wee bit edgy.'

The three old ladies frowned, shook their heads, held a case conference. Dr Ormerod changed the drugs and dosages, Sister Wood altered the regime of care, offering a drive

61

before the morning Ovaltine and a sleep after lunch. In the afternoon she would take him to the hotel, and they could all have tea together there. 'Quite a little treat,' Sister explained enthusiastically.

'Idiotic,' Michael said brutally. 'I'll have a cup of tea here on the balcony as usual. Good grief, it's not a ceremony.'

Sister Wood's face fell with disappointment. She had been looking forward to the outing. Lady Adversane was something of a celebrity at the hotel, and the occasional appearance of her crippled grandson caused an unmistakable stir, and other guests rallied around. This infuriated the patient, but Sister Wood thought it splendid of them.

'You'll enjoy meeting the young people at the Excelsior, Michael,' Dr Ormerod stated with shattering blindness. 'It's dull for you with us old fogies,' she added with more truth.

Lady Adversane thought herself neither an old fogy nor dull, and said so with acerbity. 'Whatever you may call yourself, Sybil.'

Michael supported her, 'No one would ever call you dull,' he assured her, his lips crinkling into genuine amusement. 'But the crowd in that hideously opulent place you've chosen to stay at are worse than dull.'

'Vulgar,' Lady Adversane rejoined promptly. 'The hotel and the people, I'm afraid, have changed greatly since Freddie

62

and I began coming here. A cup of tea on your balcony would be much more tolerable.'

Dr Ormerod and Sister Wood exchanged exasperated glances. Michael noticed this. He knew that look so well. He was being uncooperative, a bad patient. He tried to make an effort for once. All the same, he was blowed if he'd give in completely and go to their horrible hotel. 'I'll tell you what,' he suggested, 'we'll all have tea in the place – what's it called, the Alpenrose or the Edelweiss, something like that – the tourist joint at the top of the chair lift. Above the snow line still, I shouldn't wonder.' He cheered visibly at the prospect.

There was a small stunned silence.

'I've been meaning for days to get cracking. Now's the time. I love chair lifts.'

Sister Wood gathered her forces. 'Mr Adversane,' she protested. 'You really aren't ready for anything like that yet.'

'Oh yes, I am. Damn it, anyone can sit in a chair and be whirled up the mountainside. It's great,' he encouraged her. 'You'll love it, Sister. You look down on the tops of trees.'

Sister Wood knew she emphatically would not love looking down on the tops of trees. She felt ill herself at the thought. She had never been able to stand heights. And she had on several occasions watched people joining the chair lift. They had to snatch the chairs as they came by, and clamber in. She would hardly be able to put herself into one, let alone look after her patient. And how did he suppose he was going to do it, with one leg?

'It really isn't safe. When you're stronger, perhaps,' she argued desperately. Dr Ormerod supported her. 'I think it's a little unwise, Michael. In a week or two would be more sensible, don't you agree?'

'Nothing in it.'

'I'll join you, Michael,' Lady Adversane said infuriatingly. 'We'll leave these two old fogies to have tea in the hotel, as that's what they seem to like, and we'll go up on the mountain together in the chair lift. I'll look forward to that. I don't know why I haven't done it before. It'll make a nice change. What fun.'

Sister Wood and Dr Ormerod exchanged glances again. 'Ruth, I do think you're being rather rash,' Dr Ormerod protested. 'If Michael does insist on this little outing–' Michael winced at this description '–at his present stage of convalescence, and I think it's much too soon, myself, there really ought to be two of us to look after him.'

It was Sister Wood who was a bad color now. Michael wore an expression of straightforward fury. Two of the old ladies to look after him? Stone the crows, as Leo would say.

64

'And I don't know that I'd be able to,' Dr Ormerod's gaze assessed Michael's long frame clinically. 'I don't think I have the strength.'

'Oh, forget it,' Michael's rage was intense. 'It's not worth all the fuss and hullabaloo.' He was even more put out to hear himself sounding like a sulky schoolboy.

His grandmother was undeterred. 'I think it would be fun,' she repeated longingly. 'Do let's.'

Dr Ormerod's eyes took them all in. That evening she telephoned Sandy Drummond. 'He's not progressing as he should,' she explained to Sandy in London. 'And frankly, I'm afraid Sister Wood isn't up to it. Ruth doesn't help, either. Nor does Michael himself, to tell the truth. He queries all my decisions, disagrees with every drug I prescribe and then with the dosage. He considers me hopelessly out of date, I can see that. He may be right, of course. But if he'd stick to a regime – either his own or mine – we might get somewhere. All this chopping and changing is useless. The worst part, though, is his depression. I don't like it. I'm very much afraid it's reaching the cold inaccessible stage, where all effort seems futile. This suggestion about the chair lift is the only positive action he's taken in weeks. I couldn't sanction it – it honestly wasn't safe, you know – but that in itself was a mistake. So there it is, you see. He's out of our league, that's the problem.'

'I'll come out for a day or two,' Sandy promised immediately. Three days later he arrived, booked in at the hotel, talked to Lady Adversane and Dr Ormerod, then walked up to the clinic.

Here Sister Wood received him rapturously, escorted him to Michael's door, prepared to follow him in. 'Thank you, Sister,' he said firmly, shutting her on the wrong side.

Michael looked up. 'Good lord. Where've you sprung from?'

'Just thought I'd pop out and see how you were getting on. How are you?'

'Bloody-minded, I'm afraid. Did they send for you – the old ladies?'

'Send for me?'

'Patient being difficult.'

'Are you, then?'

'Oh, immensely. Sister Wood is probably at the end of her tether. All my fault,' he added fairly.

'Have you been driving her as hard as that?'

'I don't honestly know. Shouldn't be surprised. I've given her a pretty bad time, I expect.'

'But are you giving yourself a bad time, Mike? That's more to the point.'

Michael laughed shortly, with no amusement, 'Moderately.'

'Let's go over you,' Sandy said. He gave him a thorough examination, coupled with one of his searching sessions of cross-questioning. Then he asked, 'Still getting that tingling in your left leg?'

'Yes.'

'Still the same?'

'As a matter of fact, not exactly,' Michael admitted. They were talking about the sensations he was receiving from the leg he no longer possessed. 'It's worse, if anything. More than simply tingling. It aches a good deal.'

'Where?'

'Usually in the shin.' He shrugged. 'If it wasn't that I'm getting a bit fed up with it – especially as there's nothing to be done about it – it would be fascinating. Nothing like experiencing these oddities at first hand.' He smiled. 'My overactive phantom that won't lie down and die just yet. I don't think we need take too much notice of it, though. It's hanging around here with nothing to do that gives me too much time to pay attention to these odd aches and pains. I'm not worried about it, or anything. It'll go away in due course.'

'I haven't a doubt of it. But we'll have a good look, just the same.' He examined the results of his surgery in detail. 'Very healthy,' he said finally. 'Healing beautifully now.'

'A beautiful job,' Michael agreed.

'Reasonably competent,' Sandy admitted, with a glint in his eye. 'Glad you like it.'

'I do.' Michael grinned back. 'Believe it or not, I'm actually growing quite fond of it. Progress is being made in some directions, if not in others.'

'Glad to hear it. Well now, I'm going to put you on chlorpromazine for a week or two,' Sandy said, with a jovial self-confidence he was far from feeling. 'Tide you over this difficult patch, eh?'

Michael had not been prepared for this. He flushed scarlet, and his veins stood out. 'I'm damned if you're putting me on any bloody tranquilizer. What the hell have those silly old women been telling you?'

People who knew Sandy Drummond socially often thought him kindly, benevolent and easygoing. His colleagues and juniors knew another side, and Michael ran head-long into it now, though not for the first time. There was a hard-fought battle between them. Sandy won it. He sat in the chair on the balcony, comfortably writing out the prescription, and discussing the other half of the bargain, the area in which he had been prepared to meet Michael's wishes. He could come back to London.

'I can't stand this place,' he had protested throughout their talk. 'There's nothing to do, nothing to think about. I don't like *looking* at mountains. I like climbing them.

That's out, so what am I doing here? Let those three old dears scamper about the alpine meadows to their heart's content, collecting their interminable flora. I'll go back to London and do some work.'

On this point Sandy gave in. He went off to sell the move to Lady Adversane.

'London? Whatever for?'

'He thinks,' Sandy reported, 'that he'll do some work.'

'Nonsense. Out of the question.'

Sandy knew she was right. 'It's doing him no good here, though. So we'll have to try something else.'

'I gather you've no notion what that will be?' Lady Adversane scanned Sandy unexpectantly, rather as though he were one of her dimmer students. Sandy was becoming a little tired of being looked up and down like this, and for the first time he began to have some sympathy with Leo's opinion of the Adversanes – supercilious and altogether intolerable.

'No,' he said shortly. 'But it's evident that we must move him.'

'I fail to see why. You've no plan. I would have thought he should stay here – where you'll agree he's most suitably cared for – until you have at least formulated an alternative.'

'He's deteriorating here. He's also miserable as sin. So I'm moving him.'

69

'He'll be exactly the same in London. Or do you suppose some miraculous change will occur on crossing the channel?'

Sandy, of course, didn't suppose anything of the sort. 'I think he must be moved,' he reiterated obstinately.

'You know, I had the devil of a fight before I could move young Mike out of that damned awful clinic,' he told Leo when he took over his ward again on his return. 'And what I'm going to do with him now I've got him here I'm blowed if I know. Because Lady Adversane – mad as a hatter, I'm beginning to suspect – is right about that. He'll do no good here. But he was doing worse than no good in Switzerland. Of course, Jane was dead against the Swiss scheme all along. I ought to have listened to her.'

'What does she say now?'

'I haven't told her, Leo. I daren't. She'll be worried stiff about Mike if she knows, and her finals are only a week away.'

'We'll 'ave to think up something without 'er, sir, that's all.' Leo swung thoughtfully forward and back, patting his already substantial abdomen.

'I'm putting him into the private wing first of all, while we do a battery of tests and X rays and so on, and he sees the limb fitter and does some organized physiotherapy.'

'Private wing?' Leo was startled. 'Isn't 'e fit enough for 'Arley Street, then?'

'Oh, he'd be perfectly all right there. Of course he would. No, it's that incredible grandmother of his raising all manner of difficulties. I had enough of a battle on my hands over bringing him back to London at all, so I simply refused to enter into detailed domestic discussion on ways and means in Harley Street, and said I was putting him into the private wing. That shut her up.'

'Well, it'll be convenient.'

Sandy frowned. 'The trouble is, I'm afraid Mike's going to find himself as much out of things here as he did in Switzerland. He says he wants to work. But he can't, of course.'

'No. 'Ardly. Not yet.'

'And he'll find inactivity even harder to take, here in the hospital, surrounded by his former colleagues, if you ask me.'

'Yeah. Then 'e'd better not stay 'ere. 'E'll 'ave to go outside London. 'Ealthier, too. Now where, I wonder?'

Sandy shook his head. 'I wish I knew. If only he wasn't so alone. No family, I mean. And his friends are either here in London working, or climbing mountains in Nepal. Apart from Lady Adversane, he has no one. If only he could drop into some busy cheerful little home, with wife and kids and a routine, there'd be much less of a problem. But that house in Harley Street is nothing but a mausoleum.'

Leo was astonished. He had never visited

71

the Adversane household, but he had not supposed it to be dreary. He had imagined some sort of cross between a stately home – like Woburn, perhaps – and the Royal Society of Medicine.

'Just about what it is.' Sandy snorted irritably. 'And how would you like to do your convalescing in the R.S.M., my lad?'

'Not at all, now you mention it, sir.'

There was a silence, then Leo remarked, 'There always Midhurst, I suppose?'

'That's a possibility, Leo. I agree.'

'Nice country air. Colleagues to talk to.'

'Or, of course, come to that, there's the Cedars at Halchester. Guisborough's very good.'

''Alchester? Tim 'Errington's down there now, isn't 'e?'

'That's right. He's Trowbridge's registrar at the Accident Unit.'

'Then I'd send Mike to 'Alchester. We can pass the word along. Tim 'Errington's married now, got a young family and all. That's the domestic setup you were after.'

'You're quite right, Leo. I'd forgotten about Herrington. He and Adam Trowbridge between them can keep an eye on Mike. I'll give Adam a ring. That's the solution. Many thanks for your help.'

'Give Jane my regards. And best wishes.'

'I'd do that. She's getting panicky, poor girl.'

72

'No need. She'll do well.'

Sandy's face lit up. 'Think so? So do I, confidentially. But then I'm prejudiced.'

Me too, Leo thought. But he said nothing. What chance had a fat boy from the slums with Sir Alexander Drummond's only daughter? The idea was no more than a bad joke – and one that was not going to be told around the Central. But privately it had always struck Leo as extraordinary that Michael Adversane, who could have turned around any day he liked and collected Jane Drummond, should have chosen to break his heart over Rachel Severall instead, a flimsy blonde in search of a meal ticket. While Jane … his thoughts found a path of their own, building a dream castle for two that was totally unlike Woburn or the R.S.M. He snapped his mind brusquely into practicalities, and went to look for General Theater Sister to discuss tomorrow's lists.

4

Adam

Sandy drove Michael down to Halchester.
The chlorpromazine had done its work and
set his troubles at a distance. All he had to
do was to exist from one meal to the next.
Not that he wanted to eat anything, but at
least meals served to mark the passage of
time. When Sandy had explained about the
visit to Halchester, Michael had been
acquiescent.

'You don't know Adam Trowbridge?'
Sandy asked. 'He must have been before
your time, I suppose. He was my registrar.'

'Oh yes?' Michael was politely disinter-
ested.

'Now he runs the Accident Unit at St
Mark's, Halchester. Tim Herrington is with
him.'

'I know Tim,' Michael agreed apathetic-
ally. From his tone he was not bothered if he
never saw him again.

'Tim's on holiday at the moment, though,
and the Trowbridges have asked you to stay
with them to start with.'

Fifteen years had gone by since Adam

Trowbridge had left the Central. He stared at Michael Adversane. Sandy's godson, of course. This was the reason Adam was having him – he'd put himself out any day for Sandy. But Sandy's registrar, too, surely? This frail boy, with curls around his ears and dirty jeans? Pallid and in need of a shave? Adam's disgust was not lessened by the garments in which Michael had elected to travel. In addition to the old pair of jeans, he wore a white cotton polo-neck sweater, topped by a way-out purple poncho.

Short, square, solid, blunt-featured, with a round bumpy forehead, a smooth cap of steadily thinning blond hair and a pugnacious chin, Adam Trowbridge was, though he didn't know it, immediately recognizable as formidable. Michael's instant reaction was surprise that this surgeon had ever left the Central.

They examined one another with all the wariness of strange animals, suspicious and ready for trouble.

In the big living room at Harbor's Eye, Justin Armitage's brilliant design in brick and glass, its great windows and wide balconies open to the sea and sky at so many angles and levels, Catherine Trowbridge gave them tea. The three men, she noted with quiet amusement, who looked superficially so unlike, were unmistakably the same breed. Surgeons, of different generations, widely varying not only in appearance but in manner, they talked the same language and the years at the Central had molded them all. Catherine, herself a girl of quiet charm, perhaps a little overcorrect, who dressed expensively in gentle colors, was an apparent contrast to her ebullient and extroverted husband, considered in hospital circles to be unorthodox, unconventional, but by some extraordinary flair able to produce results where others failed. Yet, oddly enough, it was the conventional Catherine who found no difficulty in accepting this unorthodox young man dumped on them today. Adam didn't begin to come around until Sandy, fitting in a private chat out in the drive before he left, gave him a brief rundown on Michael's career. 'He'd have been R.S.O. by now, if it hadn't been for this tragedy.'

'R.S.O?' Adam stared. This senior surgical post came after years of experience as a registrar and senior registrar, and then only to a limited few already marked out for a consultant post in their teaching hospital. It was, in fact, the job for which Adam himself had been tipped in his Central days. His failure to achieve the post had not only cast a gloom over his professional life for years, but had changed the course of his career.

'Yes. Leo Rosenstein has done his term and joined Mummery's firm on the general surgical unit. You don't know Leo, of course. He's very good indeed. Mike was taking over from him.'

This was a new light on the young dropout at present stretched along the sofa in his living room. The R.S.O's post demanded more than advanced surgical techniques. Unflappability and a high degree of organization were required. So Michael Adversane, too, had had the post snatched from him, as he had thought it within his grasp. Adam experienced the first twinge of personal sympathy.

'Failing Mike, we had no one suitable, believe it or not,' Sandy was saying. 'We've had to summon Paul Robertson back from the Johns Hopkins.' He contemplated Adam's increasing surprise with wry amusement. 'Yes, I thought you were underrating him somewhat,' he commented. 'He's in a funny old state just now, but you must remember that he's had an exceptionally tough time.' He had already explained to Adam what had been the result of the mountaineering accident, why they had been forced to amputate. Now he gave him a more detailed account, told him of the failure of the Swiss convalescence. And the acute depression that had overtaken Michael there. 'Until then he was standing up to it very well. But now he's all to pieces. Only temporarily, in my opinion. In any case, you shouldn't go too much by appearances, my boy. Funny, I never used to think of you as the conventional type.'

One of Sandy's palpable hits. Adam in his turn felt about twenty-two, a student who had made a fool of himself on a ward round.

'As I mentioned, I've put Mike on chlorpromazine,' Sandy went on. 'He was very low when I went out to see him in Switzerland. We made an error in management in sending him there, I realize now. But we wanted to move him out of the Central, because the situation – as if it wasn't bad enough to start with – had been made a good deal worse by the fact that the blonde Mike had been going around with went and got herself engaged to someone else.'

'Charming. Couldn't she at least have waited?'

'That's what the entire hospital wants to know. Especially as the man concerned is a close friend of Mike's, Julian Northcott. That little episode cost Northcott the R.S.O.'s post, in a manner of speaking.'

Adam nodded. This was undeniably the Central.

'Mind you, I don't say he was a certainty for it before this. He's able, of course, but we had never quite decided about him.'

This, Adam grasped in a blinding flash of illumination, was no doubt what they had said about him. He felt elderly. 'But that clinched it?' he suggested.

'Not only that. Leo had been against appointing him in any case. He said Northcott could never handle the young men. He'd be too easily manipulated. Then this happened, a lot of people went right off him, and...'

'And you cabled the Johns Hopkins.'

'Exactly. However, to return to Mike, when I went out to Switzerland in answer to an S.O.S from old Dr Ormerod, who was looking after him, I found him in what I can only describe as a lethal depression.'

'Lethal?'

'In my judgment,' Sandy said deliberately. Their eyes met.

'Poor young devil. I'll watch it.'

'Yes. I think you should. I've given him enough chlorpromazine for another two weeks. I had a prolonged battle with him before I could get him to agree to take it. He promised me he would, though, and normally he'd keep a promise, once extracted. Now, though, I don't know.'

'I'll bear it in mind.'

'Yes. You may want to put him on something different of course. I've no doubt he'd be in favour of that. He's certainly not in favour of the present regime. Don't on any account let him juggle about with dosages and so on himself. I've had that out with him once, and he's toed the line since. But in Switzerland they couldn't manage him at all.

One reason why I brought him home. He played merry hell with poor Dr Ormerod. Of course she is old-fashioned. But very sound. Mike had no confidence in her, and whatever she prescribed, he either wouldn't take it, and prescribed something different for himself, or else he did take it, but adjusted the dose to suit his own notions.' He laughed shortly. 'Understandable, of course. I'd want to do the same in his place. But don't you let him even begin, or there'll be no end to it.' He sighed, fidgeted. 'There's one other point. I don't know precisely what drugs he's got with him. He had nothing in his room in the private wing. I confiscated the lot. But whether he collected any from Harley Street while he was there supervising his packing, I can't say. I'm afraid I haven't had the heart to challenge him a second time. I thought it would come better from you.'

'I'll take them off him, then,' Adam said flatly.

Sandy nodded. 'I'd think it a sensible precaution.'

Adam went thoughtfully back into the house, and walked firmly into Michael's room. They had put him into Adam's ground-floor study, which could be easily converted into a self-contained suite of bedroom and attached bathroom. He was already in bed, with the Sunday papers spread around him, wearing *Art Nouveau* pajamas topped by the purple poncho. Adam blinked. Michael raised a languid eye from the *Sunday Times* color supplement.

'Tim Herrington's on holiday at the moment,' Adam began, marking time. He found himself disinclined for an immediate confrontation. 'You knew him, I expect?'

'Herrington? Sandy's houseman a year or two back. Yes. Pleasant bloke. Could have been quite good if he'd concentrated, instead of giving most of his attention to tennis.'

Adam was startled. The unmistakable voice of the Central, authoritative, assured, coming from this weirdie in the fringed poncho. This was the senior registrar speaking, no doubt at all, though appearances were against it. What was more, he agreed with him.

'You're quite right. He's given up tennis now.'

'Should have given it up in his fourth year, if he was going to in the end.'

'I agree. He should.' Adam decided to quit dithering on the sidelines. 'Where are your drugs?' he asked baldly. He had never believed in treading delicately. If something had to be said, say it, with no beating around the bush.

'Drugs?' Michael looked up, not sure he'd understood.'

'Your drugs. Hand 'em over.'

He had understood. He stared at Adam. His color ebbed, then flooded. 'In my briefcase. Where they can stay.' He was curt.

'Oh no, they can't. No self-medication in this house. I'm supposed to be looking after you.'

'I'm perfectly capable of administering my own drugs. There's no question of self-medication. Sandy prescribed them.'

'That your briefcase?' Adam walked around the bed to where an expensive though slightly battered crocodile case with what looked suspiciously like gold fastenings rested against the bedside table. He picked it up, saw the gold initials. F.M.A. 'This old Freddie's?' he inquired, fascinated. He was sure it must have been. It brought the distinguished physician – who had taught Adam as a student, and had remained one of the most impressive figures he had ever encountered – straight into the room with them. It served to remind him, too, as nothing else would have done, that the unshaven disheveled boy confronting him was yet an Adversane. Come to think of it, old Freddie had been a leader of fashion in his day. But was this fashion now? Jeans and ponchos?

'Yep.' Michael was pretending to read the paper. Not succeeding, though.

'Well, I learned my medicine from him, and you'll take your drugs from me, my boy. Keys.'

Michael went still and silent. Then, unexpectedly, he gave in. 'What's the difference?' he asked – himself, rather than Adam, though. He picked up his key ring, selected a key and handed it over.

Adam unlocked the case. He was not pleased. They had avoided a battle, true, but only because young Adversane didn't care enough to have one. A bad sign. He took the drugs, locked the case, gave the keys back and settled a monosyllabic patient down for the night.

He thought about Michael on and off throughout the busy Monday that followed. How was he going to deal with him, break through the barrier of apathy, reserve and incipient dislike?

He decided to try the one interest he knew they shared. Surgery. When he returned home in the evening, and settled down with a drink before the meal, he made no inquiries as to how Michael was or how he had spent his day. Instead he launched himself immediately into an account of his own activities at the unit.

It worked. He had Michael's attention throughout. He had been missing the surgical talk he was used to. In Switzerland it had been biochemistry and general practice, with a little botany thrown in. Then back at the Central he found none of his colleagues would discuss surgery with him. If he introduced the subject they shied off clumsily. They had decided there was never going to be anymore surgery for Adversane, and to talk of it would only distress him. He was depressed enough already.

Leo alone ignored these finer points. 'You should 'ave bin in the general theater this morning,' he'd announce, breezing in with his house surgeon, shocked, behind him. 'It was a right shambles. We thought we was there to do a routine appendectomy on a fit middle-aged man, and 'e turned out to be a Makeke monkey.' He nudged his uncomfortable houseman. 'I tried to catch Mike 'ere with that when 'e was your age, but 'e wasn't wearing it. 'E knew.'

'Probably you'd told me, Leo, in the first place.'

'Oh no, I 'adn't. Because I remember thinking I'd foxed you for sure that time. And you looked at me over your mask in a supercilious manner, and said, "You mean the appendix is in the right upper quadrant, I suppose?"'

'Yes, well, I used to spend a good deal of time and energy swotting up with the object of preventing you from catching me out on occasions like that,' Michael said with a reminiscent smile. 'Of course, Leo, you know you're a superb teacher. You have this astonishing knack of galvanizing your staff into furious activity when your back's turned.'

Leo snorted. "Ear that, young Toby?' He turned back to Michael. 'Stone the crows, I 'ave the utmost difficulty in galvanising 'im into activity when 'e's under my nose, let alone when I turn my back. Signs of furious activity in future from you, Tobe.'

Toby muttered. He hadn't a notion how to take either of them.

'Any'ow,' Leo continued, unperturbed, 'on this occasion I'll admit it was totally unexpected. So we'd gone in in the wrong place, for a start. There we were in the right iliac fossa. Toby couldn't make out what was goin' on at all. 'E still 'adn't rumbled the Makeke monkey, 'ad you?'

His houseman mumbled incoherently.

'So then what 'appened?'

'The patient started hiccupping, no doubt,' Mike said.

'Correct. And why was that, young Toby?'

Toby began to give an uncomfortable account of the dangers of fiddling about looking for an appendix up by the diaphragm.

Leo interrupted him. 'At first I thought it was stuck to the diaphragm. I was in a dead panic. Thought we was going to end up with a pneumothorax.'

'Horrible thoughts you do have, Leo. I take it you succeeded in avoiding the danger?'

'Yeah, I got it down all right, thanks be.' This one sentence covered an exhibition of the rapid surgical dexterity for which Leo was well known. 'The patient's now back in the ward, confidently under the impression 'e's 'ad a routine little operation.'

Michael drank it in, while Sister Paré and the staff nurse exchanged anguished glances. 'I don't know how he can do it,' Sister Paré complained afterwards. 'He's uncouth. I'm sorry to have to say it about one of our surgeons, and I know how outstanding he is in many ways, but he's uncouth. There's no getting away from it. He knows perfectly well poor Mr Adversane is never going to be able to...' she couldn't even bring herself to finish the sentence, allowed it to die away, reiterated. 'I simply don't know how he can.'

But Michael enjoyed Leo's surgical reminiscences, and now he locked himself on to Adam's account of his own day at the accident unit, even asked a few questions. Adam was pleased. What he found less satisfactory was the fact that Michael ate almost nothing. 'Still no appetite?' he inquired. 'That'll be partly the fever, of course. And all those antibiotics Sandy was telling me about. We must watch it.'

Michael changed the subject back to the accident unit, and Adam, anxious to encourage this interest, allowed the problems of Michael's health to drop for the moment, though he had a word with Catherine about feeding the invalid up, and made a mental note to keep a careful eye on the patient's temperature.

After a few days of shared meals, Michael, although he continued to eat little, began to thaw out, and went so far as to contribute a few surgical reminiscences himself.

During the day, when Adam was at the unit, Catherine cherished him with little offerings of lemon tea, fruit juice, consommé, whipped up desserts of cream and fresh fruit. She loved having one of Adam's patients to look after. With no children, and Adam so often kept in the theater, her domestic chores were usually quickly over. She was a girl who liked to be busy, and if she had nothing to occupy her at Harbor's Eye, she would join her father in the Estate Office at Halford House and put in valuable hours on his numerous activities. But she infinitely preferred to remain at home, and Michael's presence gave her the opportunity. To her delight, he suddenly took a fancy to her lemon tea, and would swallow quarts of it. Equally suddenly, he began to communicate.

'Sandy wouldn't let me work in London,' he volunteered unexpectedly over coffee one evening, when he and Adam were alone in the big living room. 'But I think I'm perfectly capable of it. It would do me good. A damn sight more good than all these drugs. If I might be allowed to embark for once on this self-prescribing that you so much disapprove of – how would it be if I did some work here at St Mark's?'

'I don't see why not,' Adam agreed. If he were depressed himself, he knew he'd prefer to work it off. 'You can come to my clinics any time you like. If they'd interest you at all,' he added more dubiously. 'St Mark's not being by any means the Central.'

'Thank you, I'd like to. If I start work, I won't need any drugs.'

'We can always try it and see. Say you begin by coming to my rehabilitation clinic. That's varied, at least. People come from all over the place, in all stages. It's not wildly exciting, mind you. Simply a good solid series of assessments.'

'I'd like to come very much.'

'The day after tomorrow, then. At two. In the meantime, you'd better take it easy. You may find it a good deal more tiring than you expect.'

When Adam came home to have a bit of lunch and collect Michael for this clinic, he was taken aback. Gone was the weirdie in the poncho and shabby jeans. Instead, a formal young man appeared, dark suit, collar and tie. True, the shirt was a lurid pink, while the tie appeared to portray an herbaceous border in full midsummer glory, but the gesture had been made, and Adam appreciated it.

'You look about ready for one of your grandfather's rounds,' he said. 'I hope St Mark's won't be a disappointment.'

Michael answered his thoughts rather than his words. 'Did you think I was going to turn up in your clinic looking like some dropout on hash?' he inquired.

Adam had, of course. 'Of course not,' he lied.

'Though I must say I'd probably not feel much different if I was on hash,' Michael continued. 'More than time I came off the chlorpromazine.'

'One step at a time. Concentrate on getting enough lunch down you to see you through a four-hour clinic,' Adam retorted.

At the weekend he rang Sandy to report progress. 'He's very restive on the chlorpromazine,' he told him. 'He's suggested coming off it at least once a day since he arrived. Yesterday he ran quite a campaign. I can't keep him on it much longer, I don't think. He doesn't like being on drugs at all, for that matter, or even vitamin supplements and minerals. Says they all have side-effects.'

'What it honestly is, is that he resents invalidism in any form. He rejects it and drugs together.'

'Yes, I'd say you're right. Well, early days, I suppose. He's only been to one clinic at St

90

Mark's so far. But we have undoubtedly made an advance, you know. He tidied himself up superbly for the clinic. Shows he can, if he wants to.'

'He's normally a rather smooth and fashionable young man, you know. His shirts in particular were famous – or notorious, if you prefer it – throughout the Central.'

'I'm getting old. No escaping it. I can't take all these ruffles and ponchos and Afghan coats dripping sheepskin and embroidery.'

'Mike has one of those, too.'

'My name is Rip Van Winkle.'

'Rubbish. You're young. If I can live with it, you certainly can.'

'Talking of the younger generation,' Adam said, 'how's Jane these days?'

'Just taken her finals,' Sandy said with obvious relief. 'Passed well, thank God. Starts her first house job next week. With Basil Mummery.'

'Now I really do feel old,' Adam said. 'I thought she was still at school. Jane a house surgeon? Blow me down. Well, congratulate her for me, and the best of luck in the job.'

That evening he mentioned it to Michael. 'Sandy said Jane's done well in her finals, and starts as old Mummery's house surgeon next week.'

'Good for Jane.' Michael's face lit up. 'I must ring her. I knew she'd be all right, of course, unless she completely lost her head.

But it's nice to know she's made it. Mummery, eh? Leo's on that firm now.'

'Who is this character Leo I keep hearing about? A barrow boy from the Mile End Road, did Sandy say? And on Lord Mummery's firm? Can this be the Central I knew and loved?'

Michael grinned. 'Leo's all right,' he said. 'Tremendously able. Happy to let him carve me up any day.'

A tribute indeed. Adam was impressed.

'Good clinician too,' Michael added. 'I didn't know just how good until I was ill myself. But Leo could come in, take one look, and make me comfortable inside five minutes when the rest of them had been fiddling about unsuccessfully for hours.'

'A great gift,' Adam agreed. 'Your grandfather had it.'

'So I've always been informed.' Michael nodded. Then he pounced. 'Did you tell Sandy I was coming off the chlorpromazine?'

'We discussed it. He wasn't much in favour.'

'So I suppose that's the end of that. You'll line up behind him smartly.' Michael gave Adam a cold glance that Freddie Adversane himself couldn't have bettered. Leo would have recognized it, though, as unmistakably Michael's.

'Not necessarily,' Adam retorted. 'I'm quite prepared to bring an open mind to bear.'

Michael regarded him skeptically.

'Listen, Mike, I'm an independent sort of chap. One reason why I'm out here at Halchester,' he added recollecting another aspect of the past. Even apart from his failure to achieve the R.S.O.'s post, he'd very likely never have made it onto the staff at the Central. He'd offended too many pundits. 'If you can convince me that it's sensible for you to stop the drug – O.K., then we'll stop it.'

'I should never have gone on it. I'm sure of that. It's true that I was very depressed in Switzerland. But after all, it was a perfectly normal depression. I've got to go through it sometime. No good thinking I'm going to readjust to life as it's going to be from now on without being depressed about it, after all. It's not exactly the sort of change in circumstances one takes with gay abandon, is it?'

'No,' Adam said briefly.

'I think I would have brought myself satisfactorily out of it without drugs if I'd been allowed to deal with it my own way. What I wanted to do was simply to come back to London and put in some work. Only lectures and demonstrations, that type of thing. I'd soon have been in a more civilized frame of mind then. But Sandy wouldn't hear of it. He bullied me forcibly into doing what he said. I let him, because I knew I was in a funny old state, so I thought his judgment was more reliable than mine – apart from which I hadn't the energy to fight him. But enough is enough. Perhaps Sandy was right all along. I might find I can't manage, have to go back on the drug. All right, I accept the possibility that the experiment may be a failure. I'd still like to find out. Another thing, I want to stop taking a sedative at night. Makes me so heavy and dopey in the morning.'

'One step at a time.'

'Surely it could do no harm to try stopping them both? For a few days, at least. You know, I would rather value feeling like myself again. I haven't done for months. Packed too full of drugs. Look, I've no leg, no more future in surgery – or so they say – no job. I can't begin to adjust to all this, because no one dares let me try. Damn it, I've forgotten what I'm like unmedicated. At least let me be in a position to go in search of myself.'

This got home to Adam. He understood his reaction at once. Perhaps they had been overprotecting him. At any rate, he decided, let him try it out his way. 'All right,' he agreed. 'You win. We'll try it. You may have to pay the price, but that's up to you.'

Michael gave him his sudden smile. 'Thanks,' he said. 'What a relief. Let's start now, shall we? No sedative tonight.'

'Blast you, I suppose so.' Adam was uneasy. 'You may have a bad night.'

'Then I can read a book.'

He was to run through a number of the Trowbridges' books in the nights that followed. Adam, who often saw his light on when he came back from night calls, tried without success to persuade him to take the occasional sleeping tablet. One morning at five o'clock, returning from an accident call, he again saw a light in Michael's room. He went in to him. 'Hello. How long have you been awake?'

'Oh, only about an hour. Busy night?' He was reading the *Annals of Modern Surgery*, Adam saw.

'Pretty hectic, as a matter of fact. I'm starving. I'm going to make breakfast. You'd better come with me and have some.'

'O.K.' Michael swung himself into a sitting position, reached for his prosthesis, then his sticks, and followed Adam with alacrity. He was pleased to be up and about.

In the kitchen Adam dived into the refrigerator. 'Bacon and eggs,' he muttered. 'And tomatoes. And orange juice.' He assembled these on the teak counter top. 'Any use asking you to join me? I'm going to make scrambled eggs.'

'I don't think I will, thanks. I'll have some orange juice, though. Motorway crash?'

Adam, always as neat and organized in the

kitchen as he was in the theater, was putting rashers of bacon and tomatoes under the eye-level grill. 'Yes. Wet night, greasy road. Another of those multiple crashes. I don't know. They never learn.' He shook his head, turned the bacon over, broke eggs into a saucepan, and began to tell Michael what they had found on the motorway, and what had gone on in the accident unit theater between midnight and four in the morning.

Switching off the grill, he piled his plate with bacon, tomato and a mound of scrambled eggs. He reached for a small plate, and put a meagre two dessert spoons of scrambled eggs onto it. 'Get outside that,' he ordered.

Michael opened his mouth to protest, but instead put some egg into it. He didn't want it, but he'd make an effort to get it down.

Adam made tea, dumped the lot on the breakfast counter, reached for the big Italian pottery cups and saucers, and put them in front of Michael. 'You can look after the tea. Pour it for all of us when it's ready, and I'll take Catherine a cup.' He began to eat scrambled eggs rapidly. 'You can make some toast.'

'All right.'

Adam looked thoughtfully at him, when his first onslaught on the meal was past. 'You know, you're probably right about needing more exercise. That might do more for your appetite than anything else. Done any riding? That shouldn't be too impractical for a one-legged man.'

'Not a lot. Some.'

'Catherine rides a good deal. I do less. Prefer sailing. But my father-in-law mounts both of us, and I'm sure he'd find an animal for you. You could go with Catherine in the mornings. How does it strike you?'

'Frankly, with a dull thud. I'd fall off.'

'Probably. Would that matter?'

'I suppose not.'

'You'd better come along to the physios at St Mark's first, and learn how to fall. Then get yourself on horseback.'

Michael drank tea. 'I must say, I'd like to find myself in the open air actually doing something for a change, instead of lying about like a sack of very old potatoes.'

Adam finished his bacon and eggs, pushed his cup and saucer at Michael. 'More tea.' He watched ruminatively while it was poured, took his cup back. 'Done any sailing?'

'Not since I was at school.'

'What did you sail then?'

'G.P.14s.'

'Nice stable craft. I used to sail a Flying Fifteen. Gave it up when I married. Now Catherine and I sail a Dragon. I'd take you, if you like.'

'I've used up too much of your time already.' As he came to know Adam better, and to like him, Michael became steadily more conscious of the inroads he was making into Adam's all too limited personal life.

'Not to worry. Nothing I like better than mobilizing the injured. You know that.'

'In your spare time, though—'

'And in my spare time. It's all the same to me. I don't care much for domestic pursuits like gardening or mending fuses. Catherine sees to that sort of thing. And I'm not a culture vulture. I don't like theaters or concerts. No kids – it would be different if I had them. But if I'm off-duty I like to be active. I'm a limited sort of character, I'm afraid—'

'My God, so am I.' The words exploded from Michael.

'Are you?'

'And how. My painful discovery. Take away my work, and what seems to have been my only hobby, and there's nothing left. I'm at a standstill. Literally, in any case. But spiritually too.'

'Then you'd better come sailing,' Adam said phlegmatically.

'Sailing one-legged?' Michael was dubious.

'I'll look after you,' Adam said with a grin. *'And* you'd wear a life jacket. But it's a very safe sport. Far safer than driving a car, for instance.' He drank the last of his tea. 'I'm for a shower and a shave. Then I'm going back to the unit to look at the night's admissions.'

'I'd better do something about shaving, too.' They both walked through the living room. Adam watched Michael on his sticks critically.

'You're beginning to move about more confidently,' he commented. 'But you're very lopsided. You need some intensive physiotherapy. An hour a day is too little. You're fit enough to stand more.' He stopped suddenly, turned towards the big windows overlooking the harbour. 'Here,' he said.

Michael obediently joined him.

'That's *Wind Song*, our Dragon. On that swinging mooring there by the catamaran. Just ahead of the blue boat.'

'Oh yes, I see.'

'Tide table.' Adam reached across to the built-in bookcase the length of one wall that housed a good deal besides books, and extracted a small folder from alongside the telephone directories. 'High water about midday tomorrow. I haven't a clinic that afternoon. So I might come home at lunch time, and we'll go for a sail.'

'I'd like that.' Michael stared out of the window at the early morning light on the water. 'Nice to be looking out at the sunrise again. I never used to mind early calls. Rather enjoyed them, in an odd sort of way. The world empty, washed and clean. Only a few busy people about, all occupied. I'm glad you got me up.'

Adam looked at him, as an idea struck him. 'You're staying up, Mike. Get dressed, and you can come and see my admissions with me. Intensive Care Unit.'

'Are you sure?'

Adam nodded. 'Get dressed,' he repeated. 'Ten minutes.'

When Adam came downstairs again, shaved and changed into a sober dark suit instead of the corduroys and sweater he'd been wearing earlier, he found Michael ready.

That day was the busiest Michael had spent since his days at the Central. They looked at the patients in the Intensive Care Unit together, then while Adam went to his office and caught up on his paperwork, Michael had a workout with the physiotherapists. This was followed, though he felt distinctly shaky, by Adam's ward round.

Adam drove them both back to Harbor's Eye for lunch. 'What about the fracture clinic?' he asked. 'You were going to come to that this afternoon. Or do you feel you've had enough for one day?'

'No, I'll come,' Michael said firmly, though in reality he felt more like lying on his bed. By six o'clock that evening, when they finally returned to Harbor's Eye, he was all in, and collapsed onto the sofa in the living room with a heavy groan that was not entirely assumed.

Adam poured him a large whiskey. 'You look as if you need it.'

Catherine informed them that there were oysters for supper. 'I thought Michael might like them, so as you were both out all day, I went down to the fisheries and fetched them.'

Adam was delighted. 'What a splendid idea. We'll all have oysters. Solely for Michael's benefit, naturally. No question of extravagant self-indulgence. And champagne, too. Can't have oysters without champagne. Some of that champagne your father gave us. We can't lose, can we? Either way, we'll have us a ball. If Mike doesn't happen to fancy his oysters, I don't mind eating them for him. And that goes for your champagne too, old boy How is your appetite? Not fully recovered, I trust?'

'I daresay I might manage to toy with a few oysters and a glass of champagne, if I give my mind to it.' Michael grinned broadly.

He was to find, as it turned out, that he could down both in considerable quantity with ease and increasing euphoria.

'Reckon you'll sleep tonight,' Adam told him.

'I should think I'll go out like a light.'

He did, and had the best night's sleep he'd

enjoyed in months. Even so, he woke with the dawn once again. Determined not to give way to the depression lying in wait for him, he dressed immediately, and let himself out into the morning.

5

Wind Song

Breakfast time at Harbor's Eye, and no sign of Michael. He was not in his room. Adam shouted for him. No reply.

'Perhaps he's in the garden. It's a perfect morning. Like summer.'

'I'll have a look.' Adam scoured the garden, shouted again. Still no reply.

'How extraordinary,' Catherine said. 'Where on earth can he be?'

'Can't imagine. He's not mobile enough to go far. I'll go upstairs, see if I can catch sight of him from the balcony.' He went up to their spacious bedroom with its wide balcony that, like the terrace below, over-looked the harbor and the shipping. His eyes searched the paths and the shoreline, to no effect.

He rejoined Catherine. 'No sign of him,' he reported. 'I think I'd better drive around the lanes, see if I come across him. He was so energetic yesterday. He may have over-done it. Gone too far, and run out of steam. Or got into difficulties. Can you hold back breakfast for a bit?'

'Yes, of course,' Catherine agreed at once. 'I hope he's all right.'

'So do I.' Adam was a little worried. He could not forget that he had acted on his own intuition, against Sandy's judgment, and taken Michael off his drugs. Had he been wrong? Had yet another sleepless night driven him to some desperate step? More likely, he tried to reassure himself, that Michael had simply been overconfident, taken himself off for some sort of walk, passed the point of exhaustion and collapsed in some unknown corner of the countryside, within easy reach but out of sight and hearing.

Adam drove slowly around the lanes near Harbor's Eye, then turned into the busier secondary road that led to St Mark's. Eventually, to his immeasurable relief, a familiar lanky figure heaved itself uncertainly out of a ditch at the roadside, raised a hand in greeting. Michael, in that damned purple poncho. Adam had never expected to be glad to see the thing. He drew up. 'Can I by any chance offer you a lift anywhere?' he asked politely.

'How kind,' Michael said with a cheerful grin. He gestured towards the ditch behind him. 'I fell off,' he explained, apparently under the impression he had made all clear.

'Fell off? Fell off what?'

'Oh – your bike, actually. I hope you don't

mind. I borrowed it. At least I suppose it's your bike? I found it in the garage.'

'That old contraption? I'm amazed to hear it's in working order.'

'It's fine. I oiled it a bit, and tightened up a few nuts here and there. And pumped up the tires, of course. No bits fell off, and there doesn't seem to be a puncture. The brakes are good. In fact, it's in a damn sight better working order than I am.' He smiled widely. 'I only intended to ride it around the garden, but I suppose I was overenthusiastic. Moving around under my own power rather went to my head. I thought I'd do a bit of exploring. Then, as I say, I fell off.'

'I don't quite see how you managed to end up in the ditch.'

'Deliberately. My main preoccupation was to fall away from the road, you see. I didn't think you'd be any too pleased, for instance, to respond to an accident call and find you had to scrape my remains off the road after a lorry had been over me.'

'No, that's not allowed,' Adam agreed.

'So I threw myself hard sideways as I felt myself going, overdid it, and landed in the ditch with the bike on top of me. Sorry to bring you out.'

'Think nothing of it,' Adam said cheerfully. In fact he was delighted to find the ex-patient so independent.

'Night calls, and then hunting the countryside for me – I knew you'd be bound to find me, though. That's why I didn't do much, except sit comfortably in the ditch waiting for you to show up. Hope I haven't mucked up your morning?'

'Only postponed my breakfast.'

Michael grinned. 'Knowing the importance of breakfast in your life, I apologize deeply.'

'You're very uppish this morning.'

'People have said that before – I'm afraid it's not simply this morning. Leo always complained about it. The truth must be that I'm naturally uppish. It must have been suppressed by the chlorpromazine. Perhaps that's why Sandy put me on it?' He raised quizzical eyebrows.

Adam decided to put him down. 'I have no doubt he was well able to handle you without the aid of drugs,' he said snappishly.

'Crawl away and die, Adversane. I suppose I'm not back at the Central, by any chance?' Michael glanced around the countryside. 'It feels extremely like it. And in some very junior capacity, too.'

'Let's get the bike.' Adam climbed down into the ditch and heaved it up, then into the back of his estate car. He slammed the door, and looked at Michael. 'Can you get yourself into the car, or do you want a hand?'

'I'll be O.K., thanks.'

Adam observed him. 'Your balance is

quite good. A bit more intensive physiotherapy, and you won't need your sticks.
Then you can really begin to move around
and go places.' He got into the car himself,
and drove back to Harbor's Eye, where they
settled down to a late breakfast.

Catherine had prepared grapefruit for
them. Michael started on his with more
interest than he usually showed at meal-
times, but followed it only by a slice of toast,
refusing offers of bacon or cornflakes.

'There's another half grapefruit in the
frig,' Catherine suggested. 'Would you like
that?'

'Well–'

'You would.' She fetched it. 'I was keeping
it for you anyway. I thought you might have
it for a mid-morning snack.'

'This is a mid-morning snack,' Adam said,
glancing at his watch. 'I'm off in five
minutes precisely, Mike. You'd better get
yourself shaved.'

'I intended to.' Michael was nettled. 'Nor
am I proposing to come to St Mark's in my
poncho.' He stared at Adam, sniping with
his eyes.

'Sorry. I didn't intend to nag. I have every
confidence in you.'

'That I doubt.'

'Oh, Mike, I–'

'You treat me like a highly suspect houseman in his first pre-registration post.'

107

Adam's jaw dropped.

'No doubt it's very good for me. And no doubt I've brought it on myself. But I'm not exactly accustomed to being regarded as an erratic potential dropout.'

'Look, I–'

'I'm not complaining, you know. Merely observing and commenting. Observing myself, mainly, I suppose.'

They looked at one another.

'Forget it,' Michael added. 'It's of no importance. I'll get shaved, as you say.' He left the room.

Adam looked at Catherine, and grinned hugely. 'The patient is now fully convalescent,' he said.

That afternoon Adam and Michael went sailing. Michael returned tousled and enthusiastic. They had spun for mackerel, and when Catherine presented his fish to him, poached and served with gooseberry sauce and lemon, he demolished it almost as rapidly as Adam ate his. The following morning he announced he would take Adam's bicycle to St Mark's in the back of the car, and transport himself to Harbor's Eye after his session in physiotherapy. 'All right,' Adam agreed imperturbably, though he had his doubts.

'I'll fetch the bike. Meet you in the drive,' Michael said.

Adam gave Catherine a thumbs up sign,

went out to the drive. Surprisingly quickly, Michael appeared on the bicycle. Adam heaved it into the back of the Volvo and they set off.

Somewhat to his own surprise, though nothing would have induced him to admit this, Michael made it back to the house on the bicycle. Admittedly, he collapsed at once into a deck chair on the terrace, feeling as though his bones were cotton wool.

Catherine saw him arrive and took a mug of Complan out to him – he was still on this twice daily – and had to wake him. He had dropped off to sleep immediately, the wind from the sea ruffling his hair. Catherine stood for a moment watching him. He had a strong face, she thought, though marked still by illness, showing lines of pain, deep clefts from nostril to mouth, sunken eyes. Even so, he was astoundingly handsome. Dark curling hair, dark eyebrows, long dark lashes, straight nose, wide sculptured mouth, cleft chin. Girls must have surrounded him at the Central, she was sure of that. Why had he had to pick this one girl out of them all, who had let him down when he needed her?

'Mike,' she said gently. 'Complan.'

He woke at once. 'What? Oh, Complan.' He took it from her. 'Thanks, Catherine. You'll put some flesh on me yet.'

'I wish I could bring you something you'd enjoy.'

'Not to worry, duckie. Things are improving. I enjoyed the grapefruit yesterday, for instance. And the mackerel. Pleasant change, that was.' He spooned up Complan disinterestedly.

'There isn't anything particular you'd like, is there? Because if so, you have only to say, you know.'

He shook his head. 'Nothing I'm nursing a secret passion for, thanks all the same. Don't muddle me up with pregnant mums.' He grinned at her, with laughter in his eyes that she had never seen before.

'I don't think I'm exactly likely to do that,' she said tartly. 'Even in your charming poncho.'

'Jane's poncho, in fact,' he said absent-mindedly.

'Jane?' Surely the girl had been called Rachel.

'You know Jane. Sandy's Jane.'

'Oh.' Catherine digested this somewhat surprising information. 'She gave it to you?'

'When I was in the Central, and I was feeling too feeble to climb in and out of my dressing gown.' He fingered its folds. 'I must give it back to her, I suppose. But I've become rather attached to it. It's very comfortable.'

Catherine passed this discovery on to Adam. 'Jane's, is it?' he said. 'I must say, I'd rather see it on her than on Michael, if one of them must wear it. Though frankly I am not sold on ponchos. Jane's, indeed? I wonder what Sandy thinks?'

'What, of Jane in a poncho?'

'No. No, I didn't mean that. Though that too is an interesting speculation.' This conversation took place while Adam himself was changing into jeans, sweater and oil-skins. He and Michael were to fit in a brief sail before supper.

It was mid-May, and the days were longer now. They were able to sail in the morning before breakfast or in the evening. Suddenly a new life had begun for Michael. He soon ceased to be content to be a passenger in *Wind Song,* and in a day or two he was handling the jib sheet, while in a week or two he was eyeing the helm with longing.

Adam gave in and allowed him to helm the boat for the odd half hour, though he kept up a scathing commentary. But to Michael, reared in the hard school of the Central's theaters, this was no more than the expected accompaniment to learning a new tech-nique, and its effect was simply to put him on his mettle.

By this time Tim Herrington had returned from his holiday. Before they met at the accident unit, Michael knew himself bitten by the sailing bug, and this was the first thing he told Tim.

'Is that what it is? I expected to find a pale

invalid, and here you are, tanned and all stations go.'

'You should have seen me a couple of weeks ago. Or rather, you shouldn't.'

'You've lost weight, of course.'

'Rapidly putting it all back.'

'Come and stay with us and you'll put some more back. My mother-in-law runs a superb restaurant, and we mostly eat there.'

Michael began to protest. He must cease imposing on everyone. Either Adam or Tim. He was fit enough to be independent, and he would find a hotel.

Tim looked him over. 'No imposition. But if you genuinely want to be independent, you can still come to Long Barn. Nan's restaurant is on the ground floor, she lets rooms on the first floor, while Jenny and I and the kids have a flat in the attics. Come along and meet Nan, anyway, and you can fix it up between you, if you decide in favor.' They arranged that Michael should come for dinner the next day. 'I should warn you Nan charges the earth,' Tim added. 'All the costing was worked out by Dad's accountants. He organized Nan into running the restaurant in the first place.' He explained that his mother-in-law's finances had been in a bad state when her husband died. 'He was Justin Armitage, of course, the architect for the university.'

'And Harbor's Eye,' Michael contributed.

112

'Yes, that's right, it's one of his few private houses. He knew Sir John Halford over the university, you see, and he persuaded him to do a house for Catherine and Adam when they married – Sir John's wedding present, I think. Anyway, Dad says Justin Armitage may have been a world-famous architect, but he was a financial imbecile. If Nan hadn't been able to run it at a profit, she'd have had to sell Long Barn. Because that's all Justin left her.'

The next evening Michael went along there and met Jenny, Tim's wife, and her mother, Nan Armitage, together with what seemed like half a hundred others. Nan appeared to know all her customers by their first names, and then there were dozens of luscious Austrian girls who did the waiting and cleaning. Later, he was to sort them out and find there were four, but on that first evening Long Barn absorbed him into its own mad whirl of countless individuals all circulating furiously. Nan took him up the great oak staircase, open to the roof beams, to the first floor, and gave him a choice of rooms. 'Nearly every room has its bathroom,' she explained, 'and you can have a sitting room as well if you like. There's no rush on at present.'

'Yes, I'd like a sitting room.'

'You'd better have the two big rooms at the North end. They're very pleasant. Tim's parents always use them when they come, but they're in the States now.'

They looked at the rooms, and Michael arranged to take them from the beginning of the following week.

When he told Adam and Catherine there was an outcry.

'I can't impose on you both indefinitely.'

'But we love having you,' Catherine assured him warmly.

He remained adamant.

'He's right, you know,' Adam told Catherine afterwards. 'Though I'm genuinely sorry to see him go. I never thought I should be. When he first came I was wondering if I could hang on until Tim's return, or whether I'd have to give in and plonk him in the Cedars. But I'm glad to see him ready to take up life on his own. Very good sign. I must get on to Sandy and tell him.'

'Your lad's going great guns,' he said to Sandy the next evening. 'He's moved on from us to Long Barn with the Herringtons. He's very active, rides my old bicycle all over the countryside, comes sailing with me – nearly every day, badgers me to go out in the dawn, if I can't get away at any other time. It's nice to have an enthusiastic crew. He does fairly arduous physiotherapy at St Mark's each day. He's got his appetite back, and he's off all drugs.'

'Thank you, Adam. I thought you might

pull it off. I was very worried about him, otherwise I don't think I would have inflicted him on you in the state he was in.'

'He's pulled it off himself.'

'With your backing. He wouldn't have succeeded unaided. Taking him sailing, are you? I hope he realizes what high-powered coaching he's having.'

He stressed this to Michael himself, who reported in by telephone from Long Barn two days later.

'Yes. Adam told me. Glad to hear it. Says he's teaching you to sail.'

'Yes. It's great.'

'I hope you realize who you're being taught by.'

'Who I'm...?'

'Olympic Gold Medalist. Trowbridge.'

'*What?*'

'Thought you might not have realized. Nearly twenty years ago, of course. He gave it up soon after he qualified. Couldn't combine surgery with Olympic standard racing. But I believe he was outstanding.'

'Olympic Gold Medal. Strewth, as Leo would say. No wonder he's twitchy when I have the helm. So he gave it up for surgery, did he? Poor bloke. And then surgery gave him up.'

'What?' Sandy barked the word.

'Well, the Central did,' Michael pointed out reasonably.

115

'One's career is not irretrievably ruined merely because one doesn't continue it at the Central.' Sandy was his most biting.

Michael was obstinate. 'For some people it is. And he's one of them.'

'Have you any evidence whatever for that extraordinary statement?'

Sandy was being very touchy. But what he had said was the truth, Michael was certain of it, and he wasn't going to back down. 'He says so himself,' he rejoined. 'When I said something about being fed up, and I mentioned that I would have been R.S.O. by now, he said immediately that he knew at first hand that losing that post was hard to accept. He said when he'd failed to get the R.S.O.'s job at the Central it had been the end of the world. Then he gave me a brisk lecture on pulling myself together.'

'I never thought it had hit him as hard as that,' Sandy said slowly. Or had he? Had he known at the time, but over the years forgotten, put it out of his mind?

'I'm sure it did,' Michael was saying. 'Still does. I've heard him say more than once that he never expected to find himself in the provinces at forty. He thinks he's failed.'

'I thought he was reasonably content, running his accident unit. Which he does supremely well.'

'Oh, content, I daresay. So am I reasonably content, learning to sail and eating stupendous meals at Long Barn. But it's hardly the success story of a lifetime.'

Sandy grunted, changed the subject. 'Time you came up for your next lot of path. tests,' he said. 'I want to make quite sure we've eliminated that infection. I'd like you to see the limb fitter, too, and the physios. You'd better come up on Wednesday and see him, spend Thursday in the laboratory.'

6

Harley Street Again

'Oh, but Michael, it's my monthly sherry party on Wednesday,' Lady Adversane protested. He had just told her that he would be coming up to Harley Street for the night, and that he wanted to invite both the Trowbridges and the Drummonds – Sandy and Jane – to dinner.

'There'll have to be a surgical contingent, then.'

'I don't know that they'll mix,' Lady Adversane murmured dubiously.

'Come off it, Gran. We're not as boorish as all that.'

'Oh no, dear, that's not what I meant at all. Sandy Drummond is a most charming man, and of course I'm very fond indeed of Jane. No doubt this Mr – er – Trowbridge, is – Trowbridge?' she broke off sharply. 'Wasn't he the one who–? No, never mind. No, dear, it's the others I'm a little doubtful about. One or two of them are distinctly – what's the expression you use? *Way out*. Yes, they're way out, Michael, you know.'

Michael did know. 'I'm afraid we've struck

119

one of Gran's sherry parties,' he told Adam and Catherine. He had previously asked them not only to dinner on Wednesday, but also to stay overnight in Harley Street. Now, of course, they tried to back out.

'What, and leave me to face them all on my own?' He made a grimace that was more realistic than he would have cared to admit.

Adam saw this. 'If that's how you feel,' he said, 'we'll come and support you.'

'You don't think it'll look a bit pushing of us?' Catherine asked uneasily, when they were alone. 'Lady Adversane doesn't seem exactly keen to have us.'

'I don't care,' Adam said firmly. 'It's Mike's home too, after all. In any case, he says he's already invited Sandy and Jane.'

He invited Leo, too. ''Oo, me? Come off it, Mike. I'd stick out like a sore thumb in that crahd.'

'Gran's sherry party? Don't worry. You're the height of convention alongside some of them. You should have heard what Grandfather used to say.'

'Nah, not them. She's got an establishment noshup laid on.'

'No, Leo, she hasn't. It's only her sherry party, and I've invited the Trowbridges for dinner, and Sandy and Jane. That's all.'

'You're out of date, mate. Invitations 'ave gorn out to all the top brass. Old Mummery's 'ad one. 'E showed it me. Engraved

120

at 'ome card.'

'Mummery?' Michael yelped.

'And all the other lords and sirs. She 'asn't 'arf gorn to town.'

Michael could believe it. It was exactly like his grandmother, who had never been known to do anything by halves. Once a decision had been taken to invite what he saw now he had rashly called a surgical contingent, it was like turning on a tap, out of which would undoubtedly pour, in an unending stream, as Leo forecast, surgical lords and sirs.

'If Mummery's going to be there, that settles it, Leo. You can't back out. You'll have to come. No one else can cope with him these days.'

'Got to go along to Lady Adversane's do now,' Mummery told Leo at the end of his ward round on Wednesday afternoon. 'Haven't had an opportunity to find out what it's in aid of. You heard any news of young Michael? Not going to be there, is he? Down in the country.'

'Yes, but he'll be there. He asked me to go along.'

'Ah. Yes. Didn't suppose you'd be going.' Tactless as ever. His present registrar raised his eyes to heaven. 'Give you a lift if you come now.'

'Thank you, sir. Adversane's considerably improved from when we last saw 'im, from what 'e says. Come up for limb-fitting and path. tests.'

'Ah. Yes. We must hope to see him stronger then, beginning to think about working again.' From his tone he had no expectation of seeing these hopes fulfilled, nor did he mince words when he met Michael, looking him up and down and remarking, 'Yes, well, must admit you look a good deal improved from when I last saw you. Made some progress, evidently. What are you going to do with yourself now, eh? Got to think about somethin' other than surgery, haven't you?'

'Quite so, Basil, but no need to rub it in just now,' Sandy objected testily. 'Allow the boy to enjoy a reasonably carefree evening, shall we?'

A reasonably carefree evening. Michael savored the phrase. Considering the ill-assorted but hair-raising eminent – not to mention highly critical – company to which he was expected to play host this evening, he thought this the last description he would have applied to the prospect before him.

'I see someone who's having a carefree evening, if you like,' Mummery pointed out, heavily avuncular and all but patting Jane on her smooth red head. He switched roles and barked at her without warning. 'Who let you out? Is there anyone left on my wards?'

'I did ask you, sir,' Jane said, harassed. It was difficult with Mummery to know when she was cast as slave and when as favourite goddaughter. 'And you said it would be all right if—'

'All right, all right. No call to be so literal, young woman. Eh?'

Leo winked at Jane, now pink in the face. Michael caught the wink. It startled him. Jane and Leo?

Lord Mummery found someone else to plague. 'Ha, Trowbridge. Long time since we've seen you here.' Here presumably referred, not to Lady Adversane's drawing room in which they all stood, but to the Central London Hospital. Certainly the company was indistinguishable.

Adam wanted to shuffle his feet and mumble, but succeeded, a little to his own surprise, in holding his head up, saying, 'Yes, it is a long time, sir. Very nice to see you again.'

Mummery hardly paused. 'Last time I saw you was at a clinico-pathological conference, if I remember rightly.' He did, as ever, remember rightly. One of Adam's more hideous memories, too, and to his fury he went scarlet. Michael observed the phenomenon, new to him, with interest.

However, Mummery having achieved his objective, relented. 'This y'r charming wife? Introduce me, boy.'

Michael concealed hilarity. The remark made his evening. 'Introduce me, boy.' He'd not forget that one, next time Adam came after him with all guns firing. In his turn he winked cheerfully at Jane, who he suddenly noticed was looking both beautiful and fashionable, in a yellow silk tunic with the latest high beaded collar and matching flared trousers, with her hair piled high. 'You look great,' he muttered, below Mummery's continuing pontifications.

She turned a radiant face. 'Do I really, Mike? How marvelous. You look pretty good yourself. How are you feeling?'

'O.K.,' he said briefly. He was not telling the entire room of the raised temperature he continued to have each evening, or of the pain in his back.

Jane did not press him. Her arms ached to go around the slight shoulders she loved so much. No one could remake his career for him, or give him back his health and strength, but here today she longed at least to offer him the comfort of the body. Instead, she stood smiling at his side, joining the lighthearted chatter.

Eventually Lord Mummery, together with most of the rest of them, departed, leaving a dinner party split down the middle. Lady Adversane at one end of the table, surrounded by chemises, average age roughly seventy-five, and Michael at the other with the surgeons. He had Catherine on one hand and Jane on the other, had found one of his elegant ruffled shirts, and was apparently back to his old form. 'Very carefree and smooth and Adversane we are tonight,' as Leo put it to Sandy. 'Any of it genuine, d'you suppose?'

Sandy hesitated. Not so Adam. 'No,' he said sharply. 'He's fed up. Worried about the path. tests. Thinks the infection is still in him, you know. He may be right, of course. Depressed about losing the R.S.O.'s post, too. Knows he'll never have that now, but hasn't come to terms with it yet. Can't blame him. Took me a hell of a time to accept the fact that I was never going to be R.S.O. at the Central.' He flushed. That was something he had not meant to blurt out over the dinner table, with Sandy sitting alertly opposite. 'You don't know how lucky you've been, mate,' he added with a sidelong grin to Leo, in an attempt to cover his confusion. But his color remained high.

'Well,' he said to Catherine later, 'I got through the evening, by the skin of my teeth. No thanks to old Mummery, either, the old devil. I feel as if I've been put through a wringer. And I'm a fit man. Mike must be flaked.'

'But why should he be? He's used to them.'

'Not in their present mood, he isn't. We

125

were both under fire tonight. Both under scrutiny by the establishment. I was the black sheep, the one they'd expelled years ago, and they looked me over for signs of the deterioration that would confirm their original opinion. Mike, on the other hand, was dear old Freddie's grandson, who was in trouble and had somehow to be rehabilitated and found a new career. But Mike doesn't want a new career. He wants the old one back.'

'And as if that wasn't enough, they all criticized his ability to manage on his new leg. I think he does tremendously well on it.' Catherine had been shocked by their attitude. From Leo upwards they had been unflattering. 'Bit dot and carry one, aren't you, mate? Not exactly a standard gait, I don't call that.'

Adam had come to Michael's support. 'Mike prefers speed and mobility to regularity at present. No doubt he'll have it all sorted out and functioning perfectly in a month or two.'

They hadn't been satisfied of course. 'You'll have to do a good deal better than that, you know,' they told him. 'Wait till Miss Herbert sets eyes on you.' They were referring to the Senior Physiotherapist.

'Still, from my point of view, it was well worth it,' Adam told Catherine. 'In at the deep end, all right, but worth it.' He shivered realistically, laughed apologetically. 'After all these years, I don't know why I care. I do, though. You know, I hadn't quite taken it in until yesterday, but there's no doubt that an Adversane can still open doors closed to anyone else. Last night was important for me ... and Mike worked it. And he did it deliberately, I'm sure of that.'

Catherine took his point at once. 'You mean that was his bread and butter letter?' she asked. 'His thank you for having me?'

'Just that. And worth a lot to me.' Laughter lurked in his eyes. 'Just as Sandy told me – only I refused to believe him at the time – in action Michael's undoubtedly smooth, you know. Unlike Leo Rosenstein, of course. Now there's the new-style consultant all right. In my day, someone like Leo wouldn't have had a hope of getting onto the staff. He's good, of course. And I must say, I liked him. And I say, what about Jane? What a dish. Gone on Mike, of course. Did you see her face light up for him? He has a special feeling of some sort for her, too, though I'm not sure quite what.'

'They reminded me of you and me,' Catherine said nostalgically. 'When you were R.S.O. at St Mark's, and I was still a schoolgirl, home for the holidays. My face must have lighted up like that for you – for simply years and years, I'm sure. And I certainly never knew what you felt for me.'

127

'You do now,' Adam pointed out factually. 'None of this would matter a row of beans if you weren't with me. You know that, don't you?'

While they were talking, Michael was touring the hospital. He had X rays of his back, which had been paining him, saw the limb fitter, and the overbearing Miss Herbert. She was, as they had all forecast, dissatisfied with his method of walking, and told him the pain in his back was undoubtedly caused by the unevenness of his gait and the inept manner in which he swung his prosthesis forward with each step, using, she assured him, all the wrong muscles. After an agonizing workout with her, he had lunch with Sandy at the Royal Society of Medicine. Sandy took one look, ordered him a large brandy. 'Get that down,' he said. 'Lunch time or not, you look as if you could do with it.'

He could. 'Thanks,' he said. 'It's Miss Herbert, you see. She put her gimlet finger on every tender spot I own, and I feel as if I'm still in spasm.'

Restored somewhat by lunch and brandy, he went on to the laboratory for innumerable tests. On his way around the departments, of course, he met many of his former colleagues. Some came up, full of pleasure at seeing him about again, exclaiming how much better he looked, asking about the results of tests, or where exactly he'd been staying and what exactly he'd been doing. Others avoided his eye, mumbled a quick greeting and scurried down corridors evasively. Still others darted behind doors or switched themselves into unlikely turnings – after all, he knew the geography of the Central as well as anyone. Julian was one of these. Presumably he imagined himself unobserved. Michael knew the action could not be intended as a snub, was almost certainly the result of mixed guilt and anxiety. Even so, he found it both hurtful and infuriating. At one and the same moment he wanted to ignore Julian's existence, while having a flaming row with him involving extreme physical violence.

A flaming row was what Sandy would like to have had with Lady Adversane, he told Adam. 'What an evening,' he said. 'I give up. How that maddening creature could have inflicted it on Mike I can't imagine. He comes back to London dreading, as I know very well, though he thinks I don't, the return to the Central, his first since his illness. And she has to give a massive bloody party for the entire surgical establishment – exactly the group I want out of Mike's thoughts at this stage of his convalescence – as well as all her blasted biochemists, and expects Mike to play host to the lot. The last evening I'd have planned for him. The woman's a menace of the first order.'

'It was a fairly alarming evening all around.'

'Mike weathered it surprisingly well. Rose to the occasion. But it exhausted him, which is just what I didn't want to happen. Today's tests and physiotherapy, after all, are no rest cure. Take him back to Halchester, Adam, as soon as he's through. Get him settled down quietly in a gentle routine. I don't want him hanging around the Central, regretting the past. Next thing we know he'll have swung right back into depression.'

'I think you may be underrating him,' Adam argued. 'It strikes me you all treat him as if he were a good deal younger and more immature than he is. After last night, of course, I can see exactly why. He's the youngest Adversane, the grandson. The child you watched grow up, whose father was a student with most of you. Aren't I right? But he's no child. He's an adult human being, with a problem. Of course he's depressed a good deal of the time at present. Any of us would be, in his position. There'd be something phoney about it if he wasn't depressed. But he can handle it. You've been trying to protect him from the full realization of what he's confronted with. But you can't. It's his life. He has to come to terms with it, and remake it himself. He has to come to accept himself, and he has to come to it the hard way. Painfully and slowly.'

'He does seem very young to me still, I must admit. You take him back to Halchester with you, anyway, and deal with him however you think best.'

'There you go again. "You take him back with you." He's not a child to be toted around the countryside at the whim of the grown-ups.'

'Damn it, I am his medical adviser.'

'Then *advise* him. Don't fix it up over his head.'

Sandy sighed. 'Perhaps I am over-protective, Adam. You deal with him in your way. He's better, as I said, away from us at the Central. We all know too much about the past, do too much looking back.'

Adam smiled. 'I'll look after him. Not to worry. In any case, I'm a fine one to read you the riot act. I'm as bossy as hell with him, as he'd soon tell you if he were with us.'

'Well, will you take him down to Halchester? Or do you want me to argue it out with him?'

'I'll tell him what we think. If I run into difficulties I'll let you know.'

But he ran into no difficulties. Michael apparently took it for granted he would drive back with them that evening. He went to sleep in the back of the Volvo, waking only when they entered the outskirts of Halchester. He had asked Adam and Catherine to have dinner with him at Long Barn, and the three of them were soon eating grilled salmon with new potatoes and peas from the garden, followed by Nan Armitage's melting gooseberry tart and cream.

'This is a good deal better than last night,' Michael remarked. 'Both the food and the atmosphere. I don't know why we always have such awful food at home.'

Catherine had been surprised by this, though Adam had barely noticed the mundane oxtail soup out of a tin, the fatty lamb cutlets that had been frozen for far too long, the watery cabbage and mashed potatoes, followed by a compote of fruit that consisted chiefly of prunes and apricots. 'I don't suppose,' she suggested, 'your grandmother has been much interested in running the house ever.'

'No. It's always been left to the housekeeper. Grandfather used to be fussy about the wine, but the food has always been pretty foul. Gran is mean with the housekeeping money, too. She's never understood about inflation. Nor did Grandfather, come to that. They kept me short of cash right through school and university – they both assumed that what did for my father in the thirties would do very nicely for me.'

'Are you solvent now?' Adam asked,

wondering if Lady Adversane – whom he was beginning, like Sandy, to label a menace – was keeping Michael short still.

'Oh yes, I've no financial problems. That at least is something I'm spared.' He grinned momentarily. 'Grandfather made half his capital over to me when I was twenty-one. Plus a terrific lecture about using the income only. When I grasped the amount he'd handed over, though, I was stupefied. Until then I'd honestly supposed we were just about scraping by.'

Adam had to laugh. 'Old Freddie scraping by is a fascinating thought.'

'I knew we owned the house in Harley Street, of course. Apart from that, I imagined we were reasonably comfortably placed, but not affluent in any way.'

'But affluent is what you are?'

'Yes, I'm afraid so.' He was a little embarrassed.

Adam was delighted. A new system of rehabilitation rose magnificently before his inner eye. 'I know the next move for you, Mike,' he said with enthusiasm. 'You want to choose yourself a damn good car. Something outstanding, that you'll enjoy driving. That'll be an experience in its own right.' As a young man Adam had driven a Lotus. He had loved the car, and it had been one of his remaining consolations when both his career and personal life had crumbled. Now a good car might well do the same for Michael, he was convinced. 'You might as well choose an outstanding make, while you're at it. I don't say a Bentley, mind, but at the same time I wouldn't be satisfied with much less.'

'You mean a Ferrari might just about do me?' Michael's blue eyes shone with amusement, and a glimmer of anticipation.

Adam's own eyes lit up in response. 'A Ferrari?' He breathed the name with reverence. 'Now there you have something. May I come with you on your search?'

The two of them spent happy hours trying out fast cars. Tim Herrington, who drove a Jaguar XJ6, joined them when he could, and pressed the claims of the Jaguar V.12 E-type automatic. 'You can drive it as an open sports in the summer, get all the fresh air you want. You won't have to wait for it to be converted for you, either. Only two foot pedals, both on the right – accelerator and brake. No clutch. You could drive it away from the showroom.' The three of them talked cars into the small hours. Catherine and Jenny Herrington commiserated with one another. 'As if it's not bad enough being married to surgeons – accident unit widows all our lives,' they said, 'now we're car widows too.'

Finally Michael settled for Tim's suggestion, and acquired a gleaming new silver E-type. He drove it back to Long Barn with a dazed expression of undeniable bliss.

'That's taken his mind off his leg and his career problems, even if only temporarily,' Adam told Catherine. 'Driving that car, he'll take on a new lease of life, if you ask me. It'll give him a boost, at exactly the right moment.'

He was right. Michael, to his amazement, found himself enjoying his summer. He ceased at last to mourn his lost limb, though it continued to give him bouts of pain, and was even beginning to be fond of his new lightweight prosthesis with its plastic socket that fitted snugly and comfortably. He rode Adam's bicycle still for exercise, walked the downs and cliffs, and sailed with Adam in *Wind Song*. He came to love the estuary and the changing light on the water. That year he watched the seasons move with new alert eyes that had time to dwell on sun, sea and sky, the hedges in their May glory and the gorse on the cliffs, sea pinks by the shore and bracken inland on the slopes.

He began to work, too. At first simply for odd outpatient sessions at St Mark's, then later for a week at a time as a locum registrar. He attended operating sessions in the accident theater as an onlooker, until he began to trust his own ability to stand in the heat for long periods.

He was beginning to think there was a chance he might return to full-time surgery, and broached the possibility to Adam, only to have it demolished.

'I know you can last out four hours in the theater,' he said. 'But you know as well as I do that doesn't mean you're fit to stand even four weeks of being on call twenty-four hours, liable to face an eight-hour stint in the theater after a full working day. You couldn't stand up to it yet, and you know it. And you're still getting that occasional evening rise in your temperature. We have to watch it still. To go back to surgery now would only end in failure. I'm sorry, Mike, but that's my considered opinion. You're not up to it. Exercise patience.'

'I'm sick and tired of hanging about without any regular employment. Don't think I don't realize perfectly well how unreasonable I'm being. Anyone else would leap at the offer of nearly a year off to live like this in the country, sailing ad lib, and so on. I'm sorry, but I can't take it. I want to get back to work, get on with building a career. It's been interrupted as it is.'

'I can't advise it.' Adam closed his lips in the thin hard line his staff recognized.

By now, Michael recognized it too. Argument was futile. In any case, he knew in his heart that Adam was right. He was not robust enough to return to surgery. He had an evening fever, and the pain still in his back – more often, too, than he let on to Adam.

136

One Saturday at lunch time, out of the blue, Jane appeared. She was driving the M.G. Sandy had given her for her twenty-first birthday. The hood was down on this September day, her skin sprinkled with a powder of freckles over a house surgeon's pallor.

'I didn't telephone,' she announced almost belligerently. 'You'd only have told me not to come. I've got the weekend. Can I stay here? Or with the Trowbridges? I can have lunch here anyway, can't I? Super meals at any time of day or night, Leo said.'

'Leo? What does he know about it?' Michael was surprisingly irritated.

Jane grinned. 'He has his methods. I expect he got it from Dad, in fact. Quite simple once you know how.'

'Sandy does know you're here, I suppose?' Michael thought he sounded like Jane's elderly aunt, but he was amazingly put out.

'No. Of course he doesn't. Why should he? I don't have to account for my actions. My free weekends are my own.'

'You ought to let your father know–' Michael began, shocked.

'Did you let your grandfather know where you went when you were a houseman?' she demanded at once. 'Hoo.' She produced the sound she had emitted almost from the cradle to indicate skepticism. 'Hoo. Not bloody likely, man.' She shook her blazing hair back and stared at him out of brown eyes whose softness belied her intransigence.

Michael knew himself helpless. He forced himself to struggle. 'Look, Jane–'

'Have lunch, then talk. I'm famished.'

He gave in, took her to lunch. At the end of the meal the Austrian waitress inquired, as usual, 'Coffee upstairs, yes?'

'Well,' Michael began.

'Yes, certainly. Thank you.' Jane was firm.

'I take it,' the girl agreed.

Jane rose. Michael, protesting, rose with her. 'Look, Jane–'

'You said you had a sitting room. I want to talk to you. It'll be nice and quiet there, won't it?'

He gave in for the second time, took her up the great open staircase to the first floor. She hung about, admiring the stairs and the rafters high above, running her fingers along the polished oak, exclaiming at the proportions of staircase, roof and huge windows overlooking the downs. People were usually impressed by Justin Armitage's conversion of the massive old barn, but Michael had known Jane too long to be taken in. She was delaying and looking around her with this detailed interest in order to give him time to climb the stairs as slowly and clumsily as he wished. Reaching the landing, he put a brotherly arm around her shoulders and gave her a friendly hug. 'You're a nice girl, J-J.'

This was a mistake. She kissed him at once. He should have been ready for it, but was not. 'Nice Mike,' she added, as she had done since she could talk. Hurriedly he limped ahead of her to the sitting room. She looked around. 'I *say*. Super.'

Michael's quarters occupied one end of the building, a room in each corner, with a bathroom between. The sitting room had windows on two walls, facing the downs to the north and the distant coastline to the west. The furniture was sparse – a low studio couch and chairs covered in tweed, with a coffee table where two pottery cups and a jug of coffee awaited them. Bookshelves and a writing table, a general impression of light and air, relaxed comfort. Inquisitive as Sandy, Jane toured the room, stuck her head out of each window in turn, then into the built-in cupboard. She found it housed elbow crutches, a walking frame, oilskins, anorak, life jacket, sea boots, and Dunlops, as well as Michael's familiar crocodile brief-case. 'The complete kit,' she said, and sniffed diagnostically. 'It's the oilskins that pong, of course.' She closed the cupboard, opened the door alongside it, which revealed his bathroom, a functional cubicle with stripped pine walls, shower, and a further door into his bedroom. Here she did momentarily hesitate. 'May I see?'

'Of course,' he said breezily. 'If I had a

sister, you'd be it. See anything you like. Sorry I can't turn over a load of socks to be darned, but they're nylon.'

Jane felt as though she had been smartly slapped. Her heart contracted and her happiness clouded dismally over. She rallied with determination. 'It's quite extraordinary,' she said brightly, 'but do you know, I don't think I've ever seen your bedroom before. It's most peculiar, when I've known you all my life, but I don't think I'd ever seen you in bed until – until that first night at the Central.'

He wanted to hug her again, tell her that she had sent him to sleep comforted. He dared not. He remained insistently and cheerfully the elder brother. 'I've seen you in bed since you were in a cot,' he reminded her firmly. Then he had to smile at one memory. 'There was one fantastic occasion, when I drove down to Dulwich with Sandy. It must have been the beginning of the holidays, I suppose. I'd been waiting for him at the Central, I know. We drove in a bit late, and you were meant to be in bed and asleep, but there you were, watching out of the nursery window and waving madly. As soon as I got out of the car you shrieked out, "Mike, Mike, look at me in my new nightie. Come and see me in my new nightie." All the adults fell about laughing, and I was fearfully embarrassed.'

'But you came and saw me just the same,' Jane pointed out. 'I didn't know what it was I'd said, but I remember the evening very clearly. I knew perfectly well, the way children always do, that the grown-ups were laughing at me, and that you were angry about it. You came up, and you were especially nice to me. I know exactly why, of course. I'd made a fool of myself.'

This time he did hug her. He could no longer stop himself. 'You were all of eight years old,' he said, remembering the small quivering body that had launched itself into his arms then, comparing it unwillingly with the warm softness of today, knowing he loved them both and always would.

'Now I'm all of twenty-four,' she said broodingly. 'The offer stands, you know.'

He jerked at once into rigidity, and turned her remark aside with a joke, as she had known he inevitably would. To cover her own hurt, she rushed on, confided her ostensible reason for coming to see him. It happened also to be genuine, though only part of the truth. 'I wanted your advice, Mike. That's why I came down. I don't know what on earth to do.'

Michael thought for one horrified moment that she was going to ask him whether she should marry Leo. It was not Leo, though, but work that was bothering her.

'I don't think I'm any good, Mike.'

He looked at her, and smiled. 'If you didn't think that in your first six months, duckie, you'd be well on the way to being a danger. You'll get it all sorted out as time goes by. Though I warn you, you'll feel like this again and again. It's part of the practice of medicine.'

She persevered. 'I mean more than that. That's what I want to talk about. If I say to anyone that I'm no good, they all make the reply you've just made. Stick it out, everyone feels like this at first.'

'Everyone does. What makes you think you're different?'

'I was a good student.'

He nodded.

'But I'm not a good house surgeon. I'm mediocre. I don't like admitting it, but I can't get away from facts. And I've somehow to find out just how good or bad I am, because otherwise I'm going through my career on Dad's reputation, with no one wanting to hurt me – or Dad. Everyone will know I'm no bloody good, and none of them will admit it. A big cover-up job for poor Jane Drummond, who's not exactly a chip off the old block.'

'Here, steady on.'

'It's horrible to be privileged, to have your path smoothed by your father's friends. No one will test me out. Instead they encourage me, take over for me when I'm in difficulties,

142

turn a blind eye. "Never mind, Jane, better luck next time. Everyone has to begin, you know." But everyone doesn't have to begin as Lord Mummery's house surgeon. That should have gone to someone better than me. When I was appointed I hoped it was because they thought I was good. It wasn't. It was because I'm a Drummond.'

'Yeah. I know.' He did. It had happened to him, too. He had been Lord Mummery's house surgeon, and he too had hoped the appointment had not been made simply because he was an Adversane. By the end of his six months he had been reassured. He had held the job down as well as anyone would have done. Now Jane had done three out of her six months, and she was not re-assured. Too early to tell? Or was she right?

'I see the people who might have expected to be Mummery's houseman in other posts, doing better than I am. They are, Mike. No good looking like that. I can recognize it dispassionately. When I was a student, it was different. I felt at home in the theater, I knew what was going on, in many ways I had the edge over the rest of them. It was hold this and swab that. I'm quite good with my hands, and I knew my way around, I honestly thought I was quite good. Well, I still like being in the theater, I'm all right in the wards and in casualty, but – but my surgical technique has more or less stood

143

still. I ought to know, Mike, you'll agree, better than most. I've watched Dad for years. And I've watched you.' Oh, how she had watched Michael. Had imagined herself assisting him in some beatific future they would share. But that was a separate problem. 'I'm hardly any better than when I started, and now I'm frightened of responsibility, because I know I won't be up to it. I'm not searching for it, hankering after it, impatient to be allowed to do more. That's how the others are. Not me.'

Michael pondered. Could she be right? 'Don't jump to conclusions, J-J,' he said. 'Just take it as it comes and reserve judgment. It may suddenly click, you know. Three months isn't long. Give it a chance.'

'But what am I going to do in three months' time?'

'Good grief, girl, you can afford to spend a year deciding. A year's nothing.'

'I suppose not,' she admitted unwillingly. 'I feel so awful, though. There are all the people I trained with, fighting for jobs, the future depending on it. And here am I – I can't turn it down if I try. They think they owe it to Dad to see me all right, and see me all right they will, however incompetent I am. It's so unfair. I'm ashamed. And yet what can I do?'

'Just your best.'

'And if it isn't good enough?'

'Look, J-J, you're not hopelessly incompetent. I know that, and so do you. You may not be going to make the sort of surgeon your father, and old Mummery – and Leo, for that matter – are. But that's not the issue. Everyone knows house surgeons who it's been clear from the beginning will never be more than adequate. After all, that's what most medical students turn into. Not geniuses at medicine or surgery. Simply useful reliable doctors and surgeons. You mustn't be too proud, love. Perhaps you're never going to be as good as your old Dad. That's not a reason for chucking it all up.'

'No. Perhaps I do expect too much. Rather cheek, when you come to think of it, to run bleating to you because after three months I see no sign of being in Dad's class. Perhaps I did imagine it would all be easier than it is. I wish I knew. But I simply can't tell. If only I was afraid of them throwing me out it would be so much easier.' She grimaced ruefully.

Michael smiled, his blue eyes alive with humor. 'They'd all laugh like drains if they heard us, you know. A Drummond and an Adversane, moaning about their unfortunate privileges.'

'You haven't done any moaning.'

'I'll remedy that at once. I too have my problems. And they're very similar to yours.'

'How can they be?'

145

'Wrapped in cotton wool. Life kept from me.'

'I wouldn't have thought–'

'If I had no money and no influence, I'd be back at work by now.'

'But surely you–'

'Oh, I've done the odd locum, attended sessions here and there. But if I was broke and had no family, they'd have found me some full-time post to keep me going, and I'd be leading a normal life instead of being told to hoard my energies and relax in the country. As it is, they won't hear of me working. And if I try to put in for a post, they'll all line up together and refuse to give me one. No one at the Central will move so much as his little finger without your father's approval. And down here they won't even blink in my direction unless Adam Trowbridge passes it – and he won't move without your father. And that's where we both came in.'

'The old man is too powerful by half,' Jane said affectionately. 'Bless him. He's such a poppet, too. What a heel I am.' She ran her hand through the thick red hair she had inherited from her old man, and looked as much like him as it was possible for a beautiful twenty-four-year-old girl to look like a plain, balding and obese man in his sixties – which was surprisingly similar.

The next morning Michael awoke with an

unusual sensation of content and joy in the day ahead. He quickly traced his highly unusual state of mind to the presence of Jane further along the corridor, and the prospect of being with her again all day. He lay thinking about her, realizing that she could easily have been alongside him, warm and loving in the flesh. He need not have snubbed her. He wished that he had not, that he had her in his arms now.

Immediately Sandy's paternal presence obtruded itself. For Michael to make love to Jane, young, impressionable, at the outset of her adult life and with a career at the Central ahead of her would be a poor return indeed for all Sandy had done for him.

So there it was. He must not on any account take advantage of Jane. She was much too young to be committed to an invalid. Jane's life was opening up. She must not be allowed to throw away her opportunities at the Central to join him wherever he succeeded in landing the odd locum, while he waited to see if they were able to eradicate the infection that continued to send his temperature climbing up each evening.

For someone who had awakened full of happiness, he had managed a good job of dissipating it in five minutes flat. This was ridiculous. Jane was spending the day with him, he had been ready to enjoy it.

Get up and dress, you fool, go on with living. One day he might be fit and healthy, and Jane still available. He thought it unlikely.

In the dining room she joined him, cheerful and wide awake in jeans and gingham shirt, sandals on bare feet. They were to spend the day sailing with Adam in *Wind Song*. Michael looked critically at her. 'Are those all the shoes you have with you? Haven't you any plimsolls?'

'No. Sorry. Should I have?'

'Can't sail in those things. You'll have to be barefoot.'

'Does it matter?'

'No.' He repented of his inexplicable bad temper. 'I use plimsolls, because I don't like wetting my gadget.' He looked her up and down. 'You'll have to do something about your hair,' he added, carping again. Its glowing beauty hung loose today, framing her face with vivid red.

'All right. Ponytail do? Or should I plait it?'

'Up to you. I should think a ponytail would do,' he assented grudgingly, then wished he wasn't suddenly being so disagreeable. What had come over him?

Jane drank orange juice, poured coffee and embarked on toast and marmalade with unruffled placidity. Inwardly she was in tears. Mike didn't want her with him. He would rather she had gone back to London the day before. He couldn't be bothered with having her around, she was nothing but a nuisance to him. He was cross and disagreeable and impatient. All he wanted was to be rid of her.

He drove her down to the harbor. Typically, he began to lose his ill-humour at the wheel of the car. And what a car. 'Mike, what a simply super car. Whatever can it be?'

'Jaguar V.12. E-type.'

Jane whistled. 'Groovy,' she said.

Michael began demonstrating the car's paces, and allowed her to listen to the music of the twelve-cylinder engine burbling gently through its four exhausts. 'It was Adam's idea,' he told her. 'He said I might as well spend my money on some real enjoyment, offset my physical handicap by driving one of the fastest cars on the road. I decided he was right. Even if I never get back to surgery, I shall earn a living somehow. So I might as well spend money now, when it does me some good. And it has done. I enjoy driving this splendid machine.'

'But you will get back to surgery, Mike. I know you will. And at the Central, too.' Jane's words came out with all the force of Sandy at his most authoritative. Michael almost believed her, she sounded so convincing.

'Let's hope so, sweetie,' he said lightly. 'Time will show. No need to worry.' He dropped his hand momentarily on hers as she sat beside him. Both of them treasured the touch for weeks afterwards.

He missed her when she had gone back to the Central. His rooms at Long Barn, filled with her warm, inquisitive, affectionate presence, for the first time felt like home, rather than some temporary lodging. His mind full of her loving outbursts – offering him her body, daring him to despair – he sat on in the room she had so firmly imprinted with her personality and thought about her own particular problem. Her future in surgery. Very likely, of course, she was right in her assessment that she would never be up to Sandy's standard. But hardly anyone was. Even Jane could be well satisfied with less. But how much less? Just how good was she?

If he'd still been at the Central he'd have been in no doubt. Almost everyone there must know, however tightly buttoned their lips. He believed Jane, though, when she said they all held back from telling her. Sandy's daughter, Lord Mummery's godchild and his house surgeon. No one was going to tell her she wasn't good enough.

7

Jane

To exist as the tolerated ineffective daughter of an outstanding father would be impossible for Jane. She was capable as well as loving, and there were many areas in which she could be fully effective. If surgery was not one of them, the sooner she discovered it the better, Michael decided – whatever he had counseled in the way of patience, when she had so unexpectedly confronted him with her fears.

How could he find out? Who would tell him? Leo?

He was damned if he was going to Leo for information about Jane.

Of course. Better than anyone. Barbie Henderson. She was Sister General Theater now, but they had learned their surgery together. They had shared many tense scenes and innumerable cups of coffee, had confided their rages, joys and despairs as they had climbed their respective ladders. Barbie was not only efficient, but observant. Nothing escaped her. She would know exactly how Jane rated.

151

He rang her.

'Mike!' Her voice was delighted. 'It's great to hear from you. How are you?'

'Very fit, thanks.'

'I *am* glad. What are you doing?'

'Sailing and locums. The thing is, I'm coming up for a routine checkup on Thursday, and I wondered if we could meet? For a coffee, say?'

'Be super, Mike. Where and when?'

'To tell you the truth, sweetie, I'd rather it wasn't anywhere around the surgical block. I don't particularly–'

'No, of course not. How about coming to the flat? That's in the staff block, but–'

'That'd be fine.'

'Top floor. Turn left out of the lift. Thursday?'

'Wednesday would be better if you could make it. Thursday's pretty full.'

'Wednesday I'm off at 4:30.'

'I could come in before I go to Harley Street. I'll have an early lunch here and drive up afterwards. Should reach you about five.'

'Do that. See you then.'

On Wednesday afternoon she rushed back, changed into her favorite trouser suit, brushed her hair out and left it flopping loosely around her chubby, engaging features. Must look casual, she told herself. Not dressed for the occasion. She didn't, unfortunately, feel casual.

She hovered at the window overlooking the staff car park. Was he still driving his Triumph convertible? She had forgotten to ask him.

He was not, of course, driving the Triumph. She gaped as the silver E-type turned in, saw Michael's dark head – saw, too, other heads turning. Only an Adversane, she thought with a spurt of rueful laughter, would imagine it possible to make an unobtrusive entrance into the staff car park at the Central in a silver E-type.

She went to the door of the flat, let him in. 'What a terrific car, Mike.' To her immense relief, he did look, just as he had said, tremendously fit. Lean and brown, his blue eyes vivid against his tan, his hair shorter but still curling irrepressibly. He looked older and tougher, she decided. No pathetic invalid here, to wring the heart.

So why was her heart wrung?

She took him into her sitting room, watching him cross it and seat himself with professional curiosity in addition to other more personal emotions. He had one stick, limped a little, but swung well from the hip and moved fast. 'You're getting around rather well.'

'Not nearly as well as Adam Trowbridge would like,' he said with a grin. 'I thought I was doing quite passably myself, but he's constantly on at me to do without a stick at all.'

'I don't see why you shouldn't,' she agreed. 'You don't seem to me to be depending on it much.'

'Only psychologically, duckie.' They smiled at one another. The phrase brought back memories of lectures and ward rounds, interminable discussions over coffee or beer.

Barbie poured tea, gave him a cup. 'Unless you'd rather have something stronger, like gin or whiskey?'

'I drink gallons of tea, Barbie, thank you. Even more than I used to, and that's saying something.'

She offered him fruit cake.

He shook his head. 'Nothing to eat, thanks. Believe it or not, I have to watch my weight. After months of forcing myself to eat, and eventually putting back the odd pound or two, I've now started putting it on at the rate of knots. It seems that eight hours sleep each night and far less exercise than I used to get will make me stout and paunchy if I don't watch it.'

'For heaven's sake, Mike, you're thin as a rake.'

'Not anymore. No snacks between meals. Thanks all the same. Don't let me stop you – you've had a hard day in the theater, not been lounging about like me.'

She took a vast piece of cake. 'I'm afraid

you couldn't stop me if you tried.'

'And how's life in the General Surgical Unit these days?'

'Fine.' She hesitated. Would he want to be told the theater gossip or not?'

'I hear Paul Robertson got the R.S.O.'s post,' he commented.

'Yes, he flew back from the States early.'

'How's he doing?'

'Oh, very well.' Better, she nearly said, than Julian Northcott could ever have done. She bit the words back in time. What was the situation between Michael and Julian? No one knew. How did Michael feel now about Rachel? And how much did he know?

'Look, Barbie, I wanted to ask you something. You'll be bound to know.'

Now he was going to ask her about Rachel. She prayed fervently for guidance. None came.

'Yes?'

'How's Jane Drummond making out?'

Barbie nearly dropped her cake. This she had not been prepared for. 'Oh lord,' she said. Her eyes met his.

'She's worried about herself,' he explained. 'Says she's no good. I can't make out whether she's set her sights too high, because of being Sandy's daughter and expecting, so to speak, to run a four-minute mile before she's learned to walk, or whether she's dead accurate. She says no one will tell her.'

Barbie began to cut her cake into tiny meticulous squares. 'Well … she's neat, of course. And organized. Very well organized indeed, just like Sandy in that.' She arranged the squares of fruit cake into neat rows of four, fiddled about picking up crumbs on her finger.

'But that's the only way she resembles Sandy?' Michael demanded.

'Well…'

'No one, not even Jane herself, expects her to be as good as Sandy for another ten years. But does she show promise?'

'She's nothing like as good as we all expected her to be, to be honest, Mike. She's competing with the cream of her year, of course. The trouble is, half a dozen of them are way ahead of her. To tell you the truth, watching her has shaken me rigid. There aren't many women surgeons, we all know that. And I was confident Jane was going to be one of the few. My money was on her from the word go. But it isn't any longer. She's still painfully slow, and she's never begun to shape up as an assistant. No anticipation, that's her trouble. She's a step behind the surgeon always, and you know how maddening that can be. Of course she's Jane Drummond – not to mention very beautiful, even behind a mask – and they're all very patient. But…' She began at last to eat her cake, looking thoroughly miserable.

'Out of the theater you know, in the wards, for instance, I believe she's very good indeed. In the theater, though, she – well, she's second rate, there's no getting away from it.'

'Thanks, Barbie. I knew you'd have the answer. I'd better tell the girl.'

'Oh God, Mike, I hope I haven't – no, I'm right. I know it, and everyone says the same. But you mustn't rely on me. She's not that bad, after all. Don't get the wrong idea. Overcautious. And on the slow side. But she'll never amount to a row of beans as a surgeon. Nothing like Sandy. Or Leo Rosenstein. Ever. Or you, even when you were still a houseman. That's what Peggy Hill says, it isn't just me. She's had twenty years of it, and she says there's no comparison.'

'It's best to know. And she seems pretty sure of it herself. She says people keep reassuring her, and they shouldn't.'

'She's so like her father in other ways, it's startling to find she isn't a born surgeon.'

'No such animal,' Michael said at once, as she had known he would. 'Surgeons are made the hard way.' The talk veered to surgical occasions they had both known.

After Michael had driven off in the E-type to Harley Street, Barbie made a face at herself in the bedroom glass. 'So much for you, my girl. He wouldn't have noticed if you'd grown two noses or been wearing hot pants. It's Jane, just as Peggy Hill always told us.' So much for Rachel, too.

Michael spent the evening with Lady Adversane. They ate a meal which astonished him by its poor quality. Had the food always been as abysmal as this?

Both of them went early to bed. The next day he had laboratory tests in the morning, lunch with Sandy, went back to Harley Street to collect his things, have a cup of tea and say good-bye to his grandmother, then made for Halchester.

That weekend when they were sailing *Wind Song* in the estuary, he mentioned the problem to Adam. 'I don't quite know what to do about Jane,' he told him.

Adam's eyes had been ranging back and forth between the wind on the water, on the sails, on the burgee at the masthead, and on the activities of other craft, some of whose helmsmen were apparently bent on the early achievement of a watery grave. He switched his gaze abruptly to Michael. What about Jane? Was he thinking about marrying her? Had he met her while he was in London and found himself in conflict? A look at his face, though, told Adam at once this was no emotional outpouring, and his glance flicked back to the masthead, the luff of the sail, and an Enterprise on collision course.

The sun shone on the water and there was a nice stiff breeze on this crisp autumn day.

158

Onshore, the trees were turning russet and gold, but the bracken was green still and waist high. Distances were hazy, but the morning mist had cleared.

Just in time the Enterprise went about. Adam held his course, remarked, 'Jane?'

'She's worried about what she should do. Career-wise. She was on about it a lot when she was down here.'

'Surely she has no need–'

'That's the trouble. Everyone tells her that, but she thinks she's no good.'

'No *good?* Sandy's daughter?'

'There you are, you see. That's what everyone says.'

'Well, is she or isn't she?'

'Probably not. That's what I unearthed when I was at the Central last week.'

'Who did you ask?'

'A girl called Barbie Henderson, who's now Sister General Theater.'

'I see. Yes.'

'Jane says no one will tell her because of Sandy. I think she's probably right.'

'So now you're wondering what you ought to say?'

'Yeah.'

'I've no doubt if Sister General Theater says she's no good it's dead accurate. All the same, you'll have to have her opinion confirmed. You can hardly tell the poor girl to chuck surgery on one opinion.'

'But who can I ask? Lord Mummery's her godfather.'

'Leo Rosenstein?'

'Leo?' Michael snapped the name back in a fashion that reminded Adam instantly of Sandy on the warpath.

'Why not? I thought he was the latest oracle.'

Michael found himself unwilling to explain why not.

'He must know,' Adam pointed out.

'They must all know,' Michael agreed. 'But will they say?'

'I'd have thought your best bet would have been to tackle this Leo character. No – er – no generation gap, for instance.'

Michael shot an amused glance at Adam. 'That may worry you. It seldom bothers me.'

'So I've noticed. I'm beginning to find it less of a handicap, I think.'

'Oh, good.' Michael was ironic.

'Probably partly due to you and your trendy gear. I'm so used to it on you, I hardly notice on others.'

'You hardly notice it on me. I'm becoming increasingly trad and conservative.'

'You could have fooled me, mate.'

Michael laughed. 'I suppose I had better talk to Leo,' he admitted. He knew there was no alternative, had probably known it all along. But now Adam had put it into words.

He left the problem, though, until a few days before his next visit to his grandmother in Harley Street. Then he rang Leo for an appointment. The fruity voice came down the line with the reassurance of long familiarity. "'Ow are yer, me old cock sparrer?' it inquired.

'O.K,' Michael said cautiously. In fact he was uneasy about his health.

'When are yer comin' up agin?'

'That's what I'm ringing about. On Thursday. I shall stay in Harley Street for a couple of days. I wondered if we could have a meal and a chat?'

Leo invited him to his flat. Or, as he phrased it, 'Come and see me pad.'

Leo's pad, like the Central itself, was in the heart of the city. Round it eddied and flowed London's traffic – vegetable lorries thundering towards Covent Garden and newspaper vans hurtling across to main line stations all night, commuters and buses all day. The packed and noisy street smelled of gas and diesel fumes, spaghetti and curries cooking, and stale beer from the pubs. The block was elderly, built around 1910, with an ancient clanking lift to transport residents to upper floors.

Leo, resplendent in a red velvet blazer, corded, and lined with black and white striped silk, let Michael in. Red carpet too, and curtains. Michael registered the lot,

161

poker-faced – or so he imagined. But Leo had known him too long and too well to be taken in. 'Me Mum ran it up out of wot she 'ad left over from the curtains,' he offered. It could even have been the truth.

'Great,' Michael said weakly. Leo had been too much for him. Score one to Leo – not for the first time.

The living room was paneled in rosewood. There were wide black leather armchairs and chesterfield, padded and buttoned, and rosewood bookcases with steel supports, a glass and steel coffee table. An electric fire with glowing coals threw its flickering gleam around the rosewood and steel hearth. Michael's gaze widened.

'All the best sultans 'ave them,' Leo told him, a shade defiantly.

'Ah yes, that's how you see yourself, is it?' Michael had recovered his cool.

'From time to time, matey. From time to time. Don't we all?'

'I daresay. I came to talk about Jane.'

Leo's face went still, then he turned his broad back and began to clink bottles and glasses. 'All in good time. Wotcher drinkin'?'

'Whiskey?'

'Whiskey it is.' He splashed generously.

'Hey, hold it.'

'You can drink that. And it'll save me poor feet.' He squirted soda less generously, handed Michael a tumbler of glass so heavily cut that cheese could have been successfully grated on it. Once again he fielded Michael's expression. 'No expense spared,' he confirmed, dead pan.

'It's all very grand and lavish, Leo.'

'I daresay. It's comfortable, I know that. And I like expensive stuff rahnd me. But is it vulgar?'

Michael blinked.

'Well, is it? I wanna know.'

'Why ask me?'

'Sort of thing you know. Go on, give. I tell you, I wanna know.'

He did, too. Michael looked around uncertainly. 'N–no,' he said slowly. 'Moneyed, of course. As you said. But–'

'Cough it up, then. What doncher like?'

'What the hell does it matter what I don't like? It's your flat, Leo. You live in it. Nothing to do with me.'

'I'm asking.'

'I suppose that thing puts me off a bit.' He gestured at the electric coals, indefatigably sending their waves of coral light out.

'I like it. And it's 'ot.'

'Couldn't you either have a real fire, or else a few bars of electricity? And does it have to be quite so baronial?' The fire was surrounded by a number of crenelated battlements, railings and knobs.

'I like it like that.'

'Well, all right then. You like it, so you have

163

it. What's it got to do with me?'

'I like to know where I stand. What else doncher like?'

'Oh, stop it, Leo.'

'Nah, c'mon.'

'If you must know, then, all those lamps.' The room was lighted by modern electrified oil lamps.'

'Give a good light.'

'They're like the fire. Phoney. If you must know what I think.'

'Yeah. I know. But I like the look of antiquity with none of its attendant discomforts. Why not?'

'Why not, indeed? And you're right there. It's a damn sight more comfortable in this place than at home. And as a matter of fact, it looks a lot better, too.' Michael's remark was genuine. The cheery warmth of Leo's pad was far more productive of well-being than the shabby grandeur of the museum-like house he'd been brought up in.

Leo had been surprised by the dinginess of the Harley Street house. Dreary, he'd thought. Old carpets, too. Priceless Persian rugs, Mummery had told him, amused. Equally happy to relate a story against himself as against anyone else, he imparted these details, including Mummery's comments, to Michael, his dark eyes defiant.

'You're right. It is dreary. Much nicer here, no doubt about it. I'd rather live in this.'

'Come off it.'

'True. For instance, I like this chair. Immensely comfortable.' He was stretched out in a superior version of a dentist's chair, black leather on rosewood, with a steel swivel base and its own footstool.

'Cost me two 'undred quid, that did. Charles Eames, they say.'

'Good God.'

'I 'eard you'd bought an E-type Jag.'

'Sure. Rather extravagant, you mean? It gives me a good deal of pleasure.'

'There you are, then.'

'Anyway, you go your own way, Leo. And why not?'

'Jane doesn't like the fire, either,' Leo said deliberately, the defiance back in his eyes.

It was Michael's turn to go momentarily still. So Jane knew this flat, had views about its furnishing. Then he took a breath, said mildly, 'I wanted to talk about her.'

'So you said. Wot abaht 'er?'

'She thinks she's no good as a surgeon. And I rather suspect she may be right. I've been making inquiries. On her behalf. She says no one will tell her. You must know.'

'Oh yeah. I know. But why should I tell you? She's got a tongue in 'er 'ead, after all. She can ask me 'erself.'

'But are you going to tell her?'

'I'm as good a judge of when to tell 'er as you are, any day.'

'How long do you propose to leave it, then?'

There was a crack in the pugnacity. 'It's difficult to start,' he admitted.

'Of course it is. But someone must. And I should have thought the sooner the better. She's worrying about what she should do next, and she literally has no idea of whether she's no good, or simply going through the usual teething troubles. She says for anyone else it would be made brutally clear – and this is true. No one would give them another job. But they'll give her one.'

'She's told you all abaht it, 'asn't she?' Leo was bitter.

'Well, for the lord's sake, Leo, she's known me all her life.'

'Is that all it is?'

'What do you mean? You sound as if you're asking me my intentions, blast you.'

'I am. I thought you were goin' to ask mine. Now I'm askin' yours.'

'At present I have none.' He was curt, but truthful. Truth was something he owed Leo.

'I thought you might 'ave.' Leo was watching him, with the eyes that always saw too much.

'No. Not now, at any rate. I admit I might have, if things had gone differently. If I was fit and at the Central.' He was astonished to hear himself confiding in Leo like this. This was what came of being truthful. Then he

166

knew there was nothing astonishing about it. It was a relief at last to come out with it, and to Leo who would know the score as well as he did himself. He would receive no jovial protestations of optimism from him, he knew that. Had he honestly come to see Leo about Jane, he asked himself suddenly. Or about his own fitness? Impossible to tell. But he'd known Leo for years now, been a colleague of his and then patient. He'd trust him with his life any day.

Like today, for instance.

'Leo,' he began.

What his voice told Leo, he could not for a moment guess. But the well-known features altered instantly. Aggression vanished, was succeeded by clinical concentration. 'Wot's wrong wiv you?' he demanded. 'Thought you was supposed to be so – fit? All an act, or what?'

'I don't know.'

'Cough it up, mate. Come clean.'

'Well, of course, my temperature's never settled properly,' he began.

'Not yet?'

'Nope.'

'What else?'

'There's this pain in my back. I have it all the time, and it shows no signs of improving. Everyone assumes it's either neurosis or else, as Miss Herbert maintains, my lop-sided totter.'

167

'You 'aven't got a lopsided totter,' Leo said forcefully. 'You walk well, whatever that obstinate old trout may tell you. Nothing ever satisfies 'er. 'Owever, it's reasonable to suppose that there might be a considerable pull still on muscles that weren't in the 'abit of bein' stretched when you 'ad two legs to call yer own.'

'I know.'

'Get a lot of pain?' Leo scrutinized him.

'A good deal.'

'Keep you awake?'

'Sometimes.'

'Let's examine you, then, Mike.'

'Oh, Leo, I'm sorry. Not in the middle of your free evening–'

'Pipe down and take y'r coat off.'

He took his coat off, and Leo went over him, as thoroughly as was his custom. 'No,' he said finally. 'Can't find nothin'.'

'I expect there's nothing to find.'

'No, yer don't. What is it, in y'r bloomin' imagination, if nowhere else? Aht wiv it.'

Michael looked dubious.

''C'mon, Mike, spit it out.'

'Oh, some tropical infection, I suppose.'

'Locked up somewhere in y'r system?'

Michael nodded.

'It could be, too. Reckon you'd better 'ave a series of X rays of your spine, Mike, as well as the path. tests. Won't do no 'arm.'

'And might reassure me, at least?' Michael

was sarcastic.

'Don't jump dahn me throat like that. Too touchy by 'alf, you are. But I reckon you know more about y'r own back than Miss 'erbert does, any day. Spinal X rays, Mike, and then we'll 'ave another talk, after we've looked at them, eh?'

'O.K., Leo. Thanks.'

'And I'll 'ave a word with Sandy for you. Now, about Jane and 'er surgery.' He paused, edgy himself for the first time.

Michael looked at him, his eyes glinting. The situation was clear as daylight. And that made two of them. 'What about your intentions, Leo?' he demanded. 'You asked about mine. I told you. So what about yours?'

Leo shrugged, spread his hands in a gesture as old as history. 'She'd never look at me.' He meant it, too, Michael could see that.

'What total nonsense.'

'Wish it was. But it isn't.'

'Of course it is.' An evening of surprises. He certainly had never expected to find himself encouraging Leo to go chasing after Jane, but he couldn't let him go on believing he had no right to do so if he wanted to. And clearly he did want to. 'You're wrong, Leo. You've got some crazy chip about the wrong background or something.'

'Wrong background, wrong race.'

'Forget it. You talk the same language,

169

you're colleagues, aren't you? You're an out-standing surgeon, and you know it. All this nonsense about coming from the Mile End Road or wherever it is – as if that was a disadvantage these days. More likely a strong point. Less boring, not out of the dreary old Harley Street circuit.'

'I'd like it if you were right. But I'm pretty certain you aren't. And it isn't the Mile End Road, while we're on the subject. I do get so tired of that. It's Cubitt Street, W.C.1 – between the Royal Free and Mount Pleasant, if you're interested. Nice little 'ouses, they are.'

'All right. All right. Anyway, wherever it is, are you going to tell her about her surgery?'

There was a silence. 'You can,' Leo said eventually. 'She asked you, thrashed it all out with you. You go ahead and tell 'er wot she wants to know.'

Michael grimaced. 'I'm quite ready to leave it to you.'

'No, you do it.'

'I've never seen her operating or assisting.'

'I know that. If you 'ad, you wouldn't be sitting 'ere asking me. You'd know.'

'Tell me, then.'

Leo told him.

Michael set his lips. Early the next morning, he telephoned Jane and made a date with her for the evening, flinching at the unmistakable joy in her response. The poor girl didn't know she had it coming to her.

Jane wanted, she said when they met, to be driven somewhere in the E-type.

'But it'll be dark quite soon.' However, the notion of showing the car off to her fired him with enthusiasm.

Jane was looking very beautiful that night. The long hours of a house surgeon had fined her down, she had lost what had been rudely referred to as her puppy fat, become instead almost willowy. She was filled with joy because she was out for the evening with Michael, and her wide mouth curved with delight. He thought she was dishy. He wanted to grab her and make love to her. Instead he brooded over the need to find enough courage to break into her unsuspecting happiness with the truth about her surgical ability. At least they'd eat first, he decided, knowing himself for a coward.

The E-type devoured the miles, and they reached Hindhead in daylight. 'We can turn off for Midhurst,' he said, 'or we could go on to the coast.'

'Oh Mike, let's. A wind from the sea. Just what I need.'

They went to Chichester. Imbued with an urge to share his enthusiasm for small boats and sailing with her, he drove first to the yacht basin. They walked around in the darkness, the wind frapping halyards rhythmically against masts and water slapping the hulls, lights glimmering across the harbor. Afterwards they drove into the city itself, and he booked a table at the Blue Anchor. Before the meal, he said he'd show her the city.

'I feel as if I'm on holiday,' Jane asserted, sniffing the air. 'What a splendid evening. Driving down through the countryside, then the yacht basin, now this old city. I feel a thousand miles from the Central and work. And what a fabulous car, Mike. It's an experience to be driven in it.'

'Glad you like it.' He took her arm. He hadn't intended to do this at all. Once it had happened, though, he could hardly shake her off as she snuggled warmly against him. Not that he had any impulse to shake her off. Quite the contrary. 'We'll go up on the walls,' he announced brusquely, disengaging at the foot of the steps leading upwards. 'Then we can look over the roofs.' Once up on the wall, he drove his rebellious hands firmly into his pockets.

Much good that did him. Jane slipped a confiding hand in alongside his. He flinched. 'Oh,' she exclaimed, undeterred. 'It's your wrong side. Sorry.' And there she was, slipping the other hand in the other pocket. Well, he'd done his best.

A wind blew in from the sea, bringing with it the chill of evening and a hint of winter. They made their way back to the Blue

Anchor, ready for the huge meal it provided.

'I had a meal with Leo last night,' Michael began.

She interrupted him. 'At his new flat? What did you think of it?' She chuckled. 'Was he wearing his red velvet?'

'Yeah. It was all very lavish. And very like Leo, I thought.'

'Yes. Isn't he sweet? I adore him.'

These amiable phrases filled Michael with irrational delight. However, 'Leo's very sound,' he said stuffily.

'Oh, absolutely.' She chuckled again. 'Except for the red velvet. That's not sound at all. But he only wears that secretly in the seclusion of his pad. Incidentally, I'm wearing your coat tonight so that I can give it back to you. You're going to need it for the winter.' His Afghan-embroidered sheepskin had been across her shoulders when she joined him.

When she had lent him her purple poncho, he had pressed the sheepskin on her in return. She had accepted it with enormous pleasure, and he had imagined it keeping her warm, even if overwhelming her. When she had appeared tonight in it, though, he had seen it looked magnificent on her.

'No, keep it,' he said. 'It suits you. And it isn't quite Halchester, let's face it. Adam would have a fit.'

'Does that weigh with you?' She was

173

surprised by his attitude. In the past he had enjoyed shocking his seniors with his colorful and often outrageous gear.

He shot her a self-deprecatory smile. 'It does a bit, you know. I don't want to let him down locally, you see. He's done a lot to push me on the medical scene there. Or maybe it's because my self-image is changing. I don't know. Anyway, you keep it. It looks great on you, but I'd be a bit suspect in it. Down there, you know, I have quite a battle to be taken seriously. They're far too apt to assume I'm young and inexperienced. What it amounts to, I suppose, is that at the Central everyone knew who I was, and as long as I was reasonably competent and hardworking, I didn't have to worry about acceptance. So I could be a rebel and have fun. At Halchester they're only too ready to write me off, so I have to brandish age and soundness at them. Foster the quiet, responsible look. You know?'

'As Leo has done always. I can see why, now.'

'Well, Leo's branching out into red velvet and striped silk just as I'm pouring myself into somber gent's suiting. All part of life's rich tapestry, duckie. You keep the sheepskin. You look gorgeous in it.'

She smiled widely. 'So do you.'

'Ah, natch,' he agreed. 'But I don't want to anymore. And it isn't entirely for the reasons

174

I've given you that I've gone off the idea of so much gorgeousness for Adversane. I don't honestly see myself like that any longer. There are all those students at the new university of Halchester, you know, loaded with trendy gear, of course. I don't belong to them at all. Adam's always on about the generation gap, but I'm far more part of his generation than theirs. I'm beginning to feel it would be a bit of a masquerade if I looked like them. What I truthfully am is a serious-minded senior registrar attending with deep concentration to his career – which needs a lot of fostering these days.'

'Is that why you've had your hair cut?'

Michael ran slightly unnerved fingers over the back of his neck, the base of which had recently for the first time been exposed to any chance draft. He felt exposed in more ways than one. It was all right for him to look Jane over, but when she studied him in this detail he wasn't sure how he felt about it. Correction. He was sure. He knew himself uneasily on probation, and this was not his customary emotion when in her company. 'I suppose so,' he agreed cautiously.

'I like it,' she said, and smiled the wide encouraging Drummond smile again. He was astonishingly relieved to see it. However, 'Never mind my hair,' he retorted ungratefully. 'We're here to talk about your future, not mine.'

'Oh, never mind that,' she said airily. This evening, she honestly didn't care tuppence about her career.

'That's what I brought you out for,' he said brutally. He didn't begin to convince himself, though when he'd rung her that morning he'd certainly believed this to be the truth.

Jane believed him all right. Her soaring hopes plummeted down. 'Very well,' she said blankly. 'My future.' She sounded so despondent that Michael had to take her hand in his. Or at least this was what he found he'd done. 'Cheer up, love. It's not as bad as that.' He found himself looking far too deeply into the brown eyes he loved, and tore his gaze away. 'Come on,' he said, getting to his feet. 'We'll have coffee in the lounge, then we can talk properly.' He ordered it, and they made their way through. They had been late with their meal, and the room was almost deserted. They found a roaring fire at the far end, with a sofa and a low table, and sat down together.

'So what about my future?' Jane asked, when she'd poured their coffee. She watched him from the half-familiar, half-unknown face of the adult she'd so recently become. Her own vivid coloring was softened by the oatmeal polo-necked sweater she wore. She appeared above all gentle, loving, approachable. As she leaned forward to pour coffee,

176

her heavy amber beads swung forward too, throwing facets of red light back to her shining hair.

He told her what she needed to know. He wanted to take her into his arms, to love her, to tell her that none of it mattered, nothing mattered so long as they could be together. He did none of this, but settled down to a detailed exposition of career openings for young medical graduates.

'So,' he said finally, 'your next move might be to do a house job in general medicine. I don't see why not.'

'I suppose so.'

'Then you will have six months each in medicine and surgery behind you.'

'Yes.'

'You sound distinctly unenthusiastic. Is all this very demoralizing?'

'Oh no. It's not that. In a way I'm relieved. After all, I was fairly certain in my own mind. Only no one would confirm what I thought. I'm glad the uncertainty is ended. It's a bit disappointing to face the fact that I was right, I admit. On the other hand, at least I can go ahead and make some plans now.'

'The Professional Medical Unit would have you.'

'I don't want to coast by on Dad's name a second time,' she rejoined sharply.

'You can't throw away that sort of pull.

Besides, your father wouldn't let you, and you can't shut him out. Least of all at this stage. It may be a bit of a blow to him, after all, to find you're going over to medicine. You can't shut him right out of your career at the same moment, simply for the sake of a whim about standing on your own two feet. Anyway, you'll have to do that on the job soon enough.'

'I suppose you're right.' She seemed so depressed that he had to put his arm around her. She must have been hit harder than she cared to admit by the destruction of her hopes.

However, her hesitation turned out to have a specific basis. 'I wasn't thinking of doing general medicine,' she told him. 'I was thinking of pediatrics.'

'It's an idea. But you'll have to do general medicine first.'

'Plenty of people don't.'

'You ought to, as you'll undoubtedly have the chance. You can do children afterwards.' He smiled suddenly. 'You might even meet me there.'

'You?' She gazed at him wide-eyed. 'Pediatrics, Mike? For you? You never said.'

'Well, I'm considering the possibility. It would be a method of keeping my options open.'

'How do you mean?'

'Adam says I'm not fit to take on a full-time surgical post. He's right, unfortunately. But I'm fed to the teeth messing about and doing locums. A week here, a fortnight there. It's very sensible, because I can take a week off between jobs, or I can have a couple of weeks simply doing odd outpatient sessions. I never need to overtire myself, and I can keep up my exercises, have plenty of rest and fresh air and so on. A well-planned regime.'

'But?' she asked softly.

'But not for me, if I can help it. No satisfaction. It keeps me from stagnating, but I miss having patients of my own and seeing them through.'

'So what are you doing, then?'

'I've organized for myself – or to be strictly accurate, Adam has organized for me – a very useful long-term locum this winter in the children's wing at St Mark's. To cover one of the registrars. An Indian girl, who's having a baby. She'll have two months off, and she wants to go part-time for another two months as well. So I'm doing it for four months in all, and we're working the hours out between us. All I have to do is start. I like kids, and I'll have this lot until next spring. I'll probably take the Diploma in Child Health then – that can't do any harm, and it'll give me another objective this winter.'

'What are the alternatives in the spring?' Jane wanted to know.

'I'm not going to be hefty enough for orthopaedic surgery again, that's for sure. I don't see why I shouldn't be fit for general surgery. But children might be better. And if it turns out – not that I see why it should – that I'm not going to have the stamina for surgery at all – Adam thinks the long hours and the night calls might be too much – then I can still go into medicine and do children. But I don't think it'll come to that.'

'It's a very sensible plan.'

'So next spring we might be meeting at the Institute of Child Health.'

'Yes.' Jane secretly formed an even firmer resolve to do children, but she said nothing to Michael about this.

He, however, assumed her sudden silence to be the result of the final abandonment of her own hopes in surgery. He took her hand comfortingly in his, to cheer her up, as he imagined. Needless to say, this worked wonders, and the following morning when he saw her radiant and content Leo raged. She was in love, and she had spent the previous evening with the man in her life. Her career might lie in fragments around her feet. But her mind was not on it.

Michael spent the morning with his grandmother. He rather felt he had been neglecting her recently – not that she seemed in any way aware of this. She had, it turned out, formed her own plan for the winter.

'I want you to come to South Africa with me, Michael. It would do you good.'

8

Spring in Halchester

'South Africa?' Michael repeated. 'You want me to go to South Africa?'

'Yes. I've been into it,' Lady Adversane explained. 'We can cruise out there, spend the winter months in the Cape, and cruise back in the spring. It will be very good for you. Good for my rheumaticky old bones, too.'

There could be little doubt of this. A horrid thought struck him. 'You haven't arranged for Sister Wood, I hope?'

'No, no. I realize that was a mistake, Michael. I'm sorry about it. I'm afraid the poor old thing is past it.'

The poor old thing was, of course, at least fifteen years younger than Lady Adversane.

'Though I did suggest to Sybil Ormerod that she might come with us.'

That let him out, Michael saw thankfully.

'I'm sorry, Gran, but I've taken a job for the winter. At St Mark's.' He told her about it.

'You don't think a complete holiday would be wiser?'

'I couldn't stand it.'

He expected prolonged argument, but she agreed at once. 'No. I wouldn't have been able to at your age. Of course I'd never have agreed to winter in South Africa either. We're very much alike, you and I.'

He thought this over, couldn't help hoping her to be mistaken.

In the disconcerting way she had, she appeared to read his thoughts. 'Over our attitude to work, if in nothing else,' she added. 'You've a great deal of Freddie in you too. It's always been a comfort to me.'

In all the years he had grown up in her shadow, she had never asked or given comfort. He regarded her uncertainly.

'I would like to winter in South Africa myself. I feel the damp these days. I'm afraid I was being selfish and committing the fatal sin of projecting my own needs onto you. Freddie always warned me about it. I'm sorry, Michael. There are two generations between us, after all. I must remember that.'

He ought to go with her. He opened his mouth to offer to reconsider his decision, work something out. She forestalled him. 'Sybil and I will enjoy ourselves on our own. You stay in Halchester and take this job if that's what you want to do.'

In early November he saw her off, and as winter came, he began to work regular hours in the children's wards at St Mark's. He found his anonymity there a considerable relief. At the Central he was labelled. Old Freddie Adversane's grandson, whose career had fallen apart after a mountaineering accident, who had to be looked after. At St Mark's he was simply that lame registrar on the children's unit – a patient of Trowbridge's, so presumably some sort of accident case. No one – other than Adam himself – imagined they had a duty to look after him, to watch him to see he didn't do too much, to ask him about what his temperature was doing, or to try to spare him night calls.

He began to read for the Diploma in Child Health, and to attend lectures at the Institute in London and the Children's Hospital in Great Ormond Street. Early in December, Dr Tara Singh, the registrar he was relieving, had her baby, and he went on duty full-time. Christmas in the hospital was hardly a novelty – he had never known it otherwise. As far back as he could remember Christmas had meant joining his grandfather in the wards at the Central. Now in the children's wards at St Mark's all was wild noisy excitement. Outside the hospital, too, there were parties. Adam and Catherine had one at Harbor's Eye, Sir John Halford, Catherine's father, had two at Halford Place – one for hospital staff (he was chairman of the management committee) and one for personal friends. Michael went with the Trowbridges to both. Tim and Jenny Herrington gave a big party at Long Barn, the Singhs gave a small party in their flat, then Nan Armitage gave a party herself at Long Barn. Finally the Drummonds gave a New Year party at Dulwich. Michael went up for it, and brought Jane down to Halchester afterwards to a party of his own at Long Barn. Her appearance there caused consternation and disappointment all around. Children's ward sisters and staff nurses took one look at the beautiful redhead Michael Adversane brought down for his party from London and knew they were not in the running and never had been.

Jane was now a house physician on the Professional Medical Unit at the Central. She was jubilant. 'Thank heaven I made the change, Mike, instead of dithering about. Of course I'm hopelessly ignorant still, but I'm progressing all the time. I don't any longer feel that almost anyone could do my job better than I can.'

Before she returned to London, Michael took her to see his children at St Mark's. She played with them, to their great enjoyment – and her own. But what he hadn't bargained for was that she did a round with him and made thoroughly useful suggestions. He should have expected this, of course. But he hadn't been at the Central since she qualified, and he had never worked with her before. The round completed his commit-

186

ment to her. As a colleague she could be as close a partner as in a personal relationship. He could hardly bear to put her on the train, to let her leave him in Halchester while she went back to the Central. Somehow he achieved the break, but his next free day saw him driving the E-type over the icy January roads to join her.

Back in Halchester again after his visit, he found himself counting the hours until it was reasonable to ring her, counting the days until it was possible to meet her again. She must not at any cost suspect what he was feeling, though. Her career at the Central was opening out. His future in surgery remained dubious in the extreme. His back was worse, though the X rays continued to show nothing. Lay off the girl, he told himself sternly, even as his hand reached out for the telephone.

Jane suspected, of course. At last she dared to hope that what she had always longed for might be beginning to happen. Michael was actually on the edge of falling in love with her.

Leo watched Jane, and raged. She was blooming, a girl happily in love. Sandy had gone to Australia and New Zealand on a lecture tour, the house in Dulwich was closed, and there was nothing to stop Jane jaunting off down to Halchester whenever she had a free weekend. These she had more regularly on the medical side than she had ever been able to as a house surgeon. Spring came, and Leo imagined her exploring the coast with Michael in the E-type.

In the early summer she brought Michael the news that she was to stay on the Professional Medical Unit for a further year. When the present six months ended, she was to be offered an appointment as senior house officer.

'That's a triumph,' Michael told her. 'A year on the unit is a recognition of your capability and usefulness, not a gesture to please your father.'

'I know. Do you realize I shall be fully registered next month, too?'

'We must celebrate.'

'Let's. I'll come down on my next weekend.'

Michael laid on a superb dinner at Long Barn for her. The Trowbridges came, and the Herringtons, and the Singhs with their new baby, put upstairs to sleep in the Herrington nursery. Everyone was hilarious and full of hair-raising hospital anecdotes – and also, as Jane saw at once, though Michael himself failed to notice it, very heavily married.

The next morning they went for a short walk along the cliffs. 'You seem to be using your stick again,' Jane said at once. 'I thought you'd stopped.'

He grinned wryly. 'So did Adam. He's not

pleased with me.'

'Can't you manage without it?' She was worried.

'Can, but don't choose to,' he said briefly.

'Why not?' She looked worried to death. Clearly she was seeing him in agony, hardly able to hobble. Michael had to reassure her, and was forced to enter into explanations.

'It's simply a label. Not to stop me collapsing to the ground, or anything like that. You needn't take it too seriously. Psychological dependence, I'm afraid.' He raised his eyebrows at her with amused self-censure. 'My psyche needs a stick, so my battered old psyche is damn well having a stick, however much Adam nags.'

She slipped her arm through his. 'Is your psyche battered, Mike?'

'A bit.' He paused. He intended to say no more, but her warmth and affection was too close and too dear to him. Suddenly he found himself admitting to her the difficulty he had not divulged to anyone. 'I'm embarrassed by limping along like some elderly invalid, you see. Clumsy. Slow. Ungainly. People look at me, and I hate it.' He flushed. 'The stick is a label. People expect me to be a bit slow and lopsided the moment they see it. I don't feel such a fool when I have it. So if it prevents me from feeling miserable and on edge half the time, it seems sensible to use it. Your father and Adam were pressing

189

tranquilizers on me at one stage. I must say I found them unacceptable. But this is my tranquilizer, and I'm hooked on it. Why should I struggle not to mind all the time?'

Jane stared at him, pain brimming from her eyes. He had given himself away.

He was not looking at her, though. He was staring out over the sea, glittering blue in the May sunlight, sparks of light flying upwards as the onshore wind met the ebb. 'It's the same thing, you know, that stops me wearing outrageous trendy gear any longer. The reason I've suddenly become so trad.' He gave her a sidelong grin, but his color remained high. 'Nothing to do, really, with presenting a conservative teaching hospital image. That's simply the line for public consumption. The truth is, I used to enjoy standing out in a crowd – childish, I admit. Now all I want is to be unobtrusive, to get by without being spotted as an oddity, a one-legged freak.' He frowned. He was pale now. What had he wanted to blurt that out for? 'You won't pass it on, J-J, will you? Because I don't think I could bear it if you did.'

As if she would dream of divulging any confidence he gave her.

Not that he wasn't being rather ridiculous, a small sane voice remarked clearly in the midst of her pain. 'There's not the slightest need to feel any of that, Mike. You don't look clumsy, or in the least like any elderly invalid. You crazy lunatic. You look terrific. You always have done, and you still do.'

'It's nice of you to say so.' Obviously he didn't believe her. 'Nice to know that some-one thinks so, anyway.'

'*True*,' she urged.

He patted her hand. 'I daresay you believe it's true. Others might think differently, though.'

'Who?'

'Plenty.'

'But who?' Jane had inherited Sandy's per-tinacity, if not his surgical skill. 'Any of us at the Central would form a queue for the chance of going out with you,' she added.

He laughed. 'Yeah, sure. I've noticed the queue stretching down Harley Street every time I go up there. And it's always stopping the traffic in Halchester, too. They're begin-ning to complain.'

'Well, I would, any day. And I'm not the only one.' But not, she thought sadly, the right one. She had been wrong to imagine he was beginning to care for her. 'I suppose you're thinking of Rachel still,' she said despondently.

'Rachel?' He was surprised. 'No, I'm not.'

She looked at him. 'I don't believe you,' she said flatly.

'Rachel was a long time ago,' he said, almost absentmindedly.

'A year and three months ago,' Jane contributed, as precisely as Sandy might have done.

'Quite so.' He was damned if he was going to explain about Rachel. He had told Jane far too much already. About this, at least, he must maintain silence. 'It was over well before that,' he heard his own voice enunciate distinctly.

'It can't have been,' Jane argued, astonished.

He was furious. 'Well, for Pete's sake, J-J, surely I ought to know?'

'Yes, of course. I'm sorry, Mike. But all the same I don't see – I mean, if so, how – well, when was it over?'

He had brought this on himself. He shrugged. 'Some time before that,' he said evasively.

Jane was looking at him in disbelief. 'But you were so upset,' she blurted out. Then it was her turn to flush. 'I mean–'

'When was I so upset?' He looked at her with naked hatred.

'In the Central. When – when she didn't come and see you. And then, when – when she did come, she – well, that upset you, too. It's no good pretending it didn't, because it did.' She wanted to run away from his enmity, to hide from the dislike she read in his tightened lips. Instead she was defiant. Just so had she confronted him as a child. Obstinately truthful.

'I was hurt in my self-esteem, if you must know,' he said with false lightness. Then his anger left him, and he took her arm. Suddenly he wanted after all to tell her this, too. That he had told no one. Had hardly even admitted to himself. 'There may not have been queues down Harley Street,' he began, 'but you'll agree I did have a certain minor reputation with birds.'

'I'll say.' Jane sounded encouragingly awed.

He pressed her arm closer. 'Yes, well – deserved or not, I had it,' he agreed with indubitable signs of smugness. 'So it was a nasty jolt to find I didn't have it any longer. It threw me for a while. That's all.'

'You mean to say it was nothing to do with Rachel personally, simply the idea of any girl not bothering?' Her voice was incredulous.

'Put like that it does sound pathetic, I admit. Not merely sounds, either. It was pathetic. But that, roughly, is how it truly was.' He gave her a sidelong look, half-amused, half-ashamed.

'I think you were a lot more upset than that,' she said bluntly.

He had been, of course. But not for any reason he could afford to explain to her.

'Nothing to do with Rachel,' he said firmly. 'Only with myself. Honestly, J-J, I dumped Rachel on Julian quite deliberately. I knew he was nuts about her, I knew she

193

was appallingly vulnerable, and I had to see her settled with someone. But what put me out, afterwards, apart from being found so lacking in masculine appeal – which hurt my vanity–'

'Not only your vanity, of course,' Jane commented.

'Eh?'

She lost patience. 'Look, Mike, will you stop treating me as if I were your nine-year-old sister fresh from junior school? I'm twenty-four, and I've done over six years in medicine. And a few men have actually taken me out and talked to me from time to time. It wasn't only your vanity that was hurt. That's obvious. I suppose you thought having your leg off was the end of your manhood, or something ridiculous like that.'

As this was exactly what he had thought, he maintained a shattered silence.

'And what about this stick you insist on using?' Jane swept commandingly on. 'Freud would have something to say about that.'

He winced visibly.

'Let me tell you, Mike Adversane, you great dope, you are as attractive to females as ever. Probably more so. And I haven't the faintest doubt of your power to seduce us in rows, if you wanted to.'

'Not in rows, darling, not in rows. That has never been my custom,' he said, finding his voice at last. He swung her around and held her to him, burying his lips in her hair that smelled fragrantly of the Mitsouko he had given her at Christmas. 'Oh J-J, you are good for me, even if totally mad. You've cured me of a nightmare, though you do have the most astonishing technique.'

He should have known, though, that there was nothing wrong with the mechanism of Jane's mind. To his alarm, she leaped unerringly to an inescapable conclusion. 'If you were in such a hurry to dump Rachel on Julian, you must have been in love with someone else.'

He stared at her, appalled.

That was where all this talk had led her.

Too late, he pulled himself together. 'No one else,' he said. 'You're wrong there.'

'Oh no, I'm not. You should have seen your expression. Who is it?'

'There is no one.' He bit his words off.

She looked at him. 'If you won't tell me, you won't.' She paused, and he thought he'd escaped. 'Why don't you go after her and get her?' came her next question, just as he'd relaxed.

'What, with no leg and no job?' The words slipped out before he could stop them.

'Oh.' She looked him up and down. 'How truly old world.' The phrase was scorching.

It was the last reaction he had expected.

'Not in the least old world,' he snapped

back. 'Common sense.'

She ignored this. 'Of course, you were brought up by your grandfather,' she said patronizingly. 'Poor Mike, I suppose it's hardly surprising if you have these quaint outmoded notions. Edwardian, really.'

He began to answer her furiously. Then he grasped her intention. More of Jane's technique. 'You're a kind girl, J-J,' he told her, and kissed her lightly on the broad forehead, scattered again with a light powdering of freckles. 'But I see through you. Thanks for trying, anyway.'

'You don't have to thank me for anything,' she said, furiously in her turn. 'It's perfectly true. Girls don't want protecting from life. They want to take what's coming. Oh, Rachel may be an exception. She is vulnerable. If that's what you call it. Personally, I would have said weak and silly. But most of us aren't so feeble. Don't you understand, if you loved a girl, she'd want to know it, not miss out on you and your love?'

'It's not what she'd rather. It's what I'd rather.'

She took a deep breath, heaved an exasperated sigh. 'Who do you think you are, Mike? Working it out by yourself like that, finding the answers to your own satisfaction? Some Victorian paterfamilias, taking all decisions for everyone, and no questions asked? I was right about your grandfather. You have some antique attitudes you've adopted from him. Women – I'm one, remember? – women aren't fragile pieces of porcelain to be protected in case they shatter into smithereens. If you were in love with me – and you may as well know I wish you were, so there – I'd want to know. I'd cope with any difficulties there might be over your health. Or what sort of job you could get. That would be for me. I'm adult, after all. You have to face the loss of your leg. No one can shelter you from it. But it doesn't mean you have to go it alone.'

With an immense effort he prevented himself from accepting the love she longed to offer. His lips were narrow, his jaw set. He was afraid to speak. He knew the wrong words would escape.

Her eyes searched his closed features, read the shuttered blank of his expression. 'I'm sorry,' she said. 'It's nothing to do with me, I know.' Nothing she could say would make any difference to him, she saw that. This was how life went. For her, he made life's meaning. But she could not touch his loneliness.

He watched the pain cross her face, saw the agony flare in her eyes. 'Don't, J-J, please. Don't look like that. I can't bear it if you do.' He held her tightly, smoothed her hair with a hand that shook.

And then it happened. Their bones melted together in union, body spoke to body, and refused to be denied.

197

'Oh God,' Jane said. 'Oh God, I thought you didn't love me at all.'

'I don't,' he said. 'Not like that.' His face narrowed. He was rigid.

'Oh no, not much,' she agreed. She was laughing, then caught her breath and kissed him, her heart naked for him to take. His body was alive against hers, his response beyond her doubt. 'I've waited all my life for this,' she told him. 'And you wanted to let me miss it?'

He turned her head and kissed her again, then broke away hurriedly. 'I've no right–' he began.

'All that guff.' She snorted disparagingly. 'You've every right. I've loved you as long as I can remember. Do you think I can simply stop? And is there any reason on this earth why I should?'

He continued to blame himself. 'You're so young to be caught like this. You don't understand. My health–'

She stopped his mouth with her hand. 'There's now. I love you. Nothing can change it. You can do what you like about it. But I shan't change. I'm here, I love you, and I shall go on loving you, whatever you say.'

He knew she would. He smiled. The shutters were down, and his eyes looked into hers with a promise he was unable to dim.

9

Leo

Now it was high summer. Bracken was green on the slopes, gorse in bloom.

'Mike seems to be spending a good deal more time in London suddenly,' Catherine remarked. Adam had just informed her that they were not sailing this afternoon. Michael had gone up to Harley Street.

Adam smiled. 'So I noticed.'

'Jane?'

'Undoubtedly.'

'I'm so glad.'

'Me too.'

But in fact Michael had gone to see Leo. 'Look, Leo,' he told him on the telephone. 'I've had enough of this. I'm not getting any better, and I've got to know where I stand. I've a chance of a surgical post at St Mark's this autumn, and I must be fit to take it and hold it down.'

They had made an appointment, and Michael spent nearly two days in the laboratories and X-ray department. Then he saw Leo, in the private consulting room he'd recently acquired in Harley Street, where he shared Lord Mummery's secretary.

'The X rays still show nothing,' he commented. He had them spread out over his desk, put them one by one in the viewing box for Michael to see. 'But your white count is up a bit.'

'I know. Well, it fits.'

'So tell me how you've bin?'

'Not too good. Nothing specific. I can't say that. But I feel tired, Leo. Tired and toxic most of the time now.'

'Fever?'

'On and off.'

''Ow much on and 'ow much off?'

Michael told him.

'Yer look fit enough,' Leo said dubiously.

'That's sailing. Sun and wind.'

'Yeah. Could be. A nice tan can be very deceptive. You're thin still.'

'Never have been overweight like some.' He stared pointedly at Leo, who chuckled.

'You want to enjoy y'r food, like me,' he suggested, patting his abdomen in the comfortable way he had cultivated since he first qualified. 'You're thinner than you used to be, yer know. And tired too, yer say. M-mm. Pain?'

Michael nodded. 'Rarely entirely free of it these days.'

''Ow much pain, and where?'

Michael showed him.

'Yeah. I see. And what does Trowbridge

200

'ave to say about all this?'

'Haven't told him,' Michael said shortly.

Leo regarded him silently. 'Yer bloody fool,' he said at length, very quietly indeed. 'Yer stoopid negligent oaf. What the – 'ell do yer mean by comin' 'ere to me and–'

'Look, Leo, I told you. I have a chance of a job down there.'

'So?'

'So he could stop me getting in. And would. I want to find out how I am without letting him in on the act.'

Leo looked at him in silence again for some minutes. 'Sandy's in New Zealand too, so yer think while 'is back's turned, yer'll pull the wool over Trowbridge's eyes and land a job, whether yer fit to take it or not. And yer think I'm goin' ter assist yer.'

Michael grinned unexpectedly, his blue eyes danced. 'You will, too, Leo. Assist me, I mean. You've got the rest a bit wrong, though. If I'm not fit I shan't attempt to take the job, so you've nothing to worry yourself about. It's simply that I don't want to raise any nasty doubts in Adam's mind at this particular stage, if it turns out that there's nothing wrong with me.'

Leo sighed. 'So I'm the mug 'oo 'as ter stick 'is bloomin' neck aht. All right then, blast you. Strip off and let's 'ave a look. But if I find anything, you needn't think I'll 'ush it up. I'm ringing Trowbridge at once and

201

tellin' 'im.' He began to examine Michael with a gentle concentrated care at variance with his rough tongue. Even so, the patient flinched more than once.

'Yeah, well, you're tender in the left upper abdomen, aren't yer? And then again round 'ere. No doubt about it.' He felt again, and Michael, lying face down on the examination couch, jerked.

'Have a heart, Leo,' he protested. 'Stop prodding at me in this abandoned fashion.'

Leo's face was heavy with thought, his lower lip protruding in a way Michael recognised as soon as he turned his head, wondering why the long silence. Leo was on to something.

Michael's own face narrowed. He had been right then. 'What have you found?' he asked sharply. He sat up, began pulling on his shirt, watched Leo warily. 'What is it, Leo?'

Leo made up his mind. 'Dunno,' he began. 'But I wouldn't be surprised, meself, if you 'adn't been right all along,' he said. 'I reckon you may 'ave 'ad this since you came back from Nepal.'

'Had what, Leo, for God's sake?'

'I'd say a perinephric abscess. It would account for all y'r symptoms. And for the fact that up to now we 'aven't bin able to find anything. A little pocket of infection, originally from y'r leg of course, and locked up for all these months. We must get a second opinion, naturally. But meself I'd say we ought to put a needle in, see what we get, 'ave it cultured. Then we may get somewhere at last.'

'You do just that, Leo.'

'I'll give the old man a ring first. We'll ask 'im to go over yer.' He picked up his telephone, and was through to Lord Mummery before Michael had fully taken in what was happening. Indeed, before he had a chance to investigate his own reactions, the Central machinery had swung smoothly into top gear. He found himself in a small room in the private wing, the property, it appeared, of a high-powered team. Sandy was in New Zealand lecturing, so Lord Mummery was in charge now, assisted by Leo. There were more tests to be endured. Scintillation counts and renal pyelograms. Leo, skilful as ever, aspirated. More laboratory tests. Always the vast army of pundits conferring over the next step, staring at him, nodding to one another. Lord Mummery, small, cherubic, downright. Leo, with his thick argumentative interjections. The intellectual rigor of the Professor of Medicine.

'The cynosure of all eyes, that's me,' Michael commented to Leo. 'At least I can be said to understand the meaning of that little phrase at last.'

Leo, who accepted nothing on trust, was

carrying out the elementary routine of taking his blood pressure. He merely grunted, listening to the pulse as it disappeared and watching the mercury. Satisfied, he grunted again, lowered his stethoscope, unwound the cuff.

'I rang Trowbridge,' he observed.

'Oh, did you? What did he say?'

'Wanted to know why you 'adn't told 'im 'ow lousy you'd bin feeling, of course. And sent you 'is regards. Said 'e'd come up and see you.'

'Oh good. Was he very annoyed?'

'Nope. 'E said "I suppose he was afraid I'd tell him he couldn't go after that job."'

Michael flushed. 'So what did you say?'

'Told 'im 'e was right. What did you expect me to say?'

'I only asked.'

'And I've told yer.' Then he relented. 'As a matter of fact, I also told 'im I thought you'd be fighting fit long before October, which is when 'e said the post was to be taken up.'

'Thanks, Leo.'

'Nothin' in it, matey. I 'ave every confidence.'

'So have I, as a matter of fact.' It was true. The trouble had been unearthed, thanks to Leo. Already, he was looking forward to picking up the threads again, going ahead with his life. Once Lord Mummery and Leo had drained the abscess, he'd be fit, able to work full-time. He'd take this job, marry Jane, watch her produce their babies. He was going to see his sons grow up, and have daughters like Jane, who would be beautiful, clever, and kind.

As though called up by his imagination, Jane herself came in, accompanying the Professor of Medicine and his registrar. 'Just thought we'd pop in and look you over,' the professor said genially. In his turn he examined Michael, eventually departing with his registrar, telling Jane to stay with the patient. 'I prescribe it,' he announced, twinkling merrily at her, winking at his registrar.

'He's in a good mood, I must say,' Michael said.

Jane was not. In fact she was terrified. She walked nervily to the window, jammed her hands into the pockets of her short white coat, stared blindly down on the traffic below.

Michael watched her. 'Don't take on, love,' he said. 'All will be well. I feel it in me bones, as Leo would say. And talking of Leo, he's bloody good. Nothing can go wrong, with him around. And Old Mummery's hand hasn't lost it's cunning, either, after nearly forty glorious years.'

'I wish you'd told me before how awful you were feeling,' Jane said.

'I haven't been feeling awful. Only tired

and a bit toxic.'

She came over, took his hand. 'Mike,' she said urgently, 'never, never, keep anything from me again. Please.'

A pathologist came in. 'I want some blood, Mike, if you don't mind. About ten ccs.'

'What in the world are you going to do with ten ccs?' Michael demanded, outraged.

The pathologist raised his eyebrows. 'You know us,' he retorted. 'Two ccs are what we need for you. The other eight are for all the papers we're writing.'

Michael thought this was only too likely to be true, and said so, with some acerbity.

Meanwhile Jane simmered.

'The girl's trying to talk seriously to me,' Michael explained to the pathologist. He had to say something, as her impatience was washing over them both in furious waves. 'Is there no privacy in this place?' he added.

'None whatever. Did something make you think there might be? You go ahead, Jane. Don't mind me.'

'It's not a joke,' Jane began indignantly. The pathologist raised an eyebrow again, went into Michael's vein.

Jane heaved an ostentatious sigh, while the pathologist drew up blood into his syringe. 'Don't mind me,' he repeated hopefully. 'You two go right ahead and talk as if I weren't here, eh?'

'Finish and get out,' Michael said firmly.

In due course this aim was achieved. The pathologist, disappointed, completed his assignment and departed.

'Seriously, Mike–'

An electrician came in. 'The bell not working, did they say?' he inquired brightly. 'Let's have a look-see.' He squatted down with a screwdriver and began to dissect the bell.

Jane emitted a strangled bellow and rushed out of the room. She met Leo outside, nearly knocked him flying. 'Keep your cool,' he advised. 'Now, wot's all this about?' He walked her slowly down the corridor, heard her out. 'Come with me,' he said. He went into the office at the end of the passage. 'I wanna "No Visitors" notice,' he stated. He took out his pen, embellished it with a number of pointed comments, initialed it, and strode back up the passage, Jane half a step behind. He fixed it to Michael's door, patted Jane on the shoulder and said, 'Go in and kiss the bloke goodnight. Three minutes, there's a good girl. No more.' He strode on down the passage and around the corner.

A tactful ten minutes later he returned, and put his head cautiously through the door. Michael was alone. 'Settled for the night?' Leo inquired.

'Yep.'

'Good. I'll see yer in the mornin'.' He

withdrew his head, went in search of the staff nurse, gave explicit instructions. As he went off down the corridor again, he encountered Lady Adversane, hovering, for once uncertain, outside Michael's door with its notice.

''E's settled for the night, Lady Adversane,' he told her. 'Did you particularly want–'

'No. No, thank you, Mr Rosenstein. Of course not. It is quite late. I just looked in, in case there was anything I – no, no. I don't want to disturb him.'

'I'll walk you home to Harley Street,' Leo heard himself offer, to his own considerable amazement.

'How very kind of you,' Lady Adversane said, producing her sudden charming smile. 'That would be nice.'

They walked along Harley Street together, an oddly assorted couple. Lady Adversane topped Leo by half a head, though he more than doubled her in inches around the circumference. He bounced along at her side, while Lady Adversane, even in her eighties, covered the pavements as though they had been moorland turf.

'Will you come in?' she inquired. 'Brandy, perhaps?'

'Very kind of you,' Leo said in turn. 'But I won't. We can both do with an early night, I expect.'

'Quite right. Quite right. I won't press you, then.'

She looked frail and lonely on the steps, and to his continuing astonishment he took her narrow shoulders in his strong plump hands, and kissed her on both cheeks. 'I think 'e'll be all right, yer know. So try not to worry more than you can 'elp. 'Ave a good night's rest, and I'll see yer in the morning'.' He set off down Harley Street in the direction of his own flat. He had a heavy day awaiting him, and he found it no easy achievement to stand by watching Jane's devotion to Michael. That Michael, once so straightforwardly his antagonist, was now not only his patient but his friend, made it no easier. He surely couldn't grudge him Jane's love, after all he'd been through, had yet to endure? He could.

Conflict might give others sleepless nights. Not Leo. He slept like a log, and was there in the theater at eight the next morning.

The Professor of Medicine came in, with Jane in attendance, and of course Lady Adversane, escorted by a cautious Director of the Biochemistry Laboratory, determined that she shouldn't make a fool of him on this occasion. Lord Mummery arrived with his registrar, Michael was wheeled in, Leo made the first incision. The actual surgery involved today was routine, almost minor, for Lord Mummery at least no more than a brief interlude. Had Michael not been Lady Adversane's grandson and Sandy Drummond's godson, Mummery would not have thought of even putting in an appearance.

For Jane, though, it was an overwhelming ordeal. When she saw Michael's body stretched out on the table, ready for Lord Mummery and Leo to begin work, she thought she would have to leave the theater. So much for all her experience. The floor swept ominously up and receded, swept up again, while cold sweat trickled over her. Somehow she controlled herself, forced herself to achieve some sort of intellectual detachment, become simply an informed observer, with a surface calm as unruffled as Lady Adversane's.

There was no sign of Michael now. Only the operation field was open to view, the strong light glaring down, Lord Mummery and Leo working as one.

'Here we are, this is what's been doing all the damage, just as you suspected,' Lord Mummery announced with satisfaction. Leo had been right, and Mummery, a generous man in his way, said so. 'Absolutely correct, m'boy, your diagnosis. Now we'll drain this nasty collection that's been accumulating here all this time, and Adversane should have no further trouble.' He released the poison that, locked in, had been causing the rise in temperature, the exhaustion and the pain, and looked across at Lady Adversane. 'Nothing to worry about now,' he said. 'We'll leave a drainage tube in, give him a good stiff course of antibiotic, and that'll be the end of that.'

Lady Adversane nodded. 'The antibiotic will be able to reach it now, and the infection can be eliminated,' she remarked instructively, more as if she were teaching students than considering her grandson's future.

'Quite so,' the Professor of Medicine agreed.

The relief was too much for Jane. Her hard-won detachment left her and she swayed dangerously. Her clothes clung damply to her and the floor was up to its old tricks. Her eyes narrowed in an attempt to focus, her breathing deepened. Through sheer willpower she stayed on her feet, the floor quieted down and eventually subsided, and then for the first time she became aware of a growing sensation of delight and happiness. Mike was going to be all right. Leo had found the trouble. Capable, reliable Leo. She smiled brilliantly at him. Since she was masked, this was apparent to no one, least of all Leo himself, busily sewing up.

The biochemist took Lady Adversane away to be restored with coffee in the laboratory, Mummery went on to the next case on his list, his registrar assisting him. Apart from Jane, only the anesthetists and Leo stood in the Intensive Care Unit, waiting for Michael to come around.

It was Leo Michael saw as he opened his eyes. He stared thoughtfully at him.

''E's around,' Leo said to Jane. She had seen for herself, of course. But as he spoke Leo pulled her in front of him so that she came into Michael's field of vision. She smiled at him. Her mask was hanging now, and even through the mists that were closing in he thought it a wonderful smile. Response shone momentarily at the back of his eyes, and he drifted off into an enveloping peace.

10

Harbor's Eye

At lunch time Adam rang Leo. His secretary answered. 'Oh yes, he said I was to find him when you rang. Would you mind holding on?'

Adam heard her chasing Leo on the internal telephone. 'General theater? Do you have Mr Rosenstein? Oh, has he? Physiotherapy? Is Mr Rosenstein with you? Right, thank you. Intensive Care? Is Mr Rosenstein there? Well, I think he's on his way. Could you grab him, and tell him I've got Mr Trowbridge waiting for him.' Various clicks and bangs ensued, then Leo's voice came on. 'Adam. Sorry to keep yer 'anging on like this. Well, our boy's doin' fine. Yeah. As we suspected, a perinephric abscess. We've drained it, and I don't think he'll 'ave no more trouble. 'E came around about two hours ago. 'E's in Intensive Care now, under sedation, of course. Yeah, do visit 'im. 'E'd like it. Tomorrow evenin' by all means. I'll be around until eightish myself – we could 'ave a word then. Right.'

The next day Adam rearranged his work,

and took off for the Central in the late afternoon.

In the Intensive Care Unit they found Leo for him, confident and welcoming. 'Glad to see yer. Mike will be, too. 'E's a bit subdued today, as you'd expect. No, not a good night. But then 'ow could 'e 'ave 'ad? It may be a small routine piece of surgery to the old man and me, but it isn't to the bloke 'oo's 'ad us tunneling nearly six inches into 'im to drain 'is little spot of bovver. Bein' a surgeon yerself is no 'elp then. 'E's sore and un-comfortable, 'e 'ad a rotten night, and 'e's tired out. Yer can sit with 'im as long as yer like, though. Yer won't get much out of 'im, but I think 'e'd like yer to be there. Yer can boot Jane out ter get some rest, too. She was up most of last night. 'E'll probably thank you for it one day, I shouldn't wonder.'

'What I can't help wondering is why people always have nasty tricky little jobs like this lined up for me?' Adam demanded. 'I sometimes think I must look as if I had a hide like a rhinoceros.'

Leo grinned. 'Sandy's doin',' he explained. 'I rang 'im in New Zealand to tell 'im what we was up to, and 'e said at once that anything 'e'd 'ave done about Mike – 'oo can be a bit obstreperous as a patient, yer know – and which I didn't feel up to doin' myself, you'd do for me. And I don't feel up to givin' Jane 'er marchin' orders. Besides

214

which, I've sent Lady Adversane 'ome, and as far as I'm concerned that's enough for one day. You barge in and throw Jane out. I'll field 'er.'

So Adam barged in and threw Jane out.

Michael gave him a contraction of the facial muscles which could be construed as a smile. Later that evening, though, he was feeling better, and began to talk a little.

'Thanks,' he said, amid pauses, 'for getting rid of Jane for me.' He lay in silence. 'She must have some rest.' Another pause. 'And get on with her job.' He stopped for some minutes. 'Tell Leo,' he began again. 'Make Jane work,' he added in a rush.

'I see what you mean,' Adam agreed. He did.

He threw Jane out twice again that evening, finally sending her off to bed. The next morning, looking in at the Central before driving down to Halchester, he passed Michael's message on to Leo.

'Yeah. 'E's right. I'll tell the lads not to make it too easy for 'er to get away. They're all lined up in droves to 'elp her. But Mike's right. She needs work now.'

'And she exhausts him when she's there.'

'Yeah. She does, doesn't she? She thinks she's 'is tower of strength, poor kid. Instead I've watched 'er wear 'im out exactly as you say, just when 'e needs all 'is reserves. 'E daren't drop 'is guard with 'er, that's the

215

difficulty. 'As to make out 'e feels better than 'e does. Whereas in fact 'e feels 'orrible. But 'e won't let on if she's around. She can look in on 'im and wave at intervals of about two hours, then go away again fast. That's all 'e needs.'

'I can understand exactly how he feels.'

'Me too. But Jane can't. She thinks she's keeping 'im goin'.'

'In a sense she is.'

'Later on she'll be vital. Just now she only tires 'im out.'

Adam went in to Michael. 'How are you?'

'Fine,' he said automatically. Then he grinned broadly. 'Lousy. Seeing it's you, I'll admit it. What a relief. My own stiff upper lip is wearing me out.'

'Do you have to be so bloody tough?'

'People look so anguished if I weaken.'

People presumably meaning Jane and Lady Adversane, Adam reflected.

'In fact I feel as though I'd been scientifically beaten up by a gang of thugs.'

Adam had to laugh. 'Not so far wrong, either, if your nomenclature is a trifle eccentric. Not perhaps how Lord Mummery and Leo are used to hearing themselves described.'

Michael's smile reached his eyes this time.

'Well now,' Adam added, 'I dropped in to let you know I'm off, down to the unit for my rehabilitation clinic. Back at the weekend.'

When he returned on Friday evening, he found Michael a good deal improved. 'You've made progress,' he said.

'Drainage tube gone. I feel almost human. Nice to see you.' He was rested and talkative, told Adam more details of his condition, accompanied by anecdotes of life in the Intensive Care Unit. Never a dull moment, he asserted.

'I see they've moved you to a cubicle now. That must be considerably more peaceful.'

'Peaceful?' He grimaced. 'Don't make me laugh, it hurts too much. Peaceful? No such word in this place. Don't know where they've all got to now, I'll admit. Normally there's not a chance to exchange two sentences together.'

'Too many rounds?'

'They never stop. There are seldom fewer than six people packed in here.'

'The hazards of being under treatment in your own hospital.'

Michael groaned. 'Too true. They mean so well, you know. Every morning, for instance, there's what I can only describe as a super teaching round. Both Professors, Medicine and Surgery. I suppose they feel that with Sandy in New Zealand, it's up to them. They travel with an army of camp followers, of course. This morning I counted twenty-four people, including sister and the physio. Then they all go out into the passage, make a noise

217

like a cocktail party in full swing. Great roars of voices and bellows of hearty laughter. Ugh.'

'Very good experience for you to discover what it's like to be on the receiving end.' Adam was unmoved.

'I'm learning, all right. I reckon I'll never be quite the same on a ward round again.'

'No harm in that.'

'And it's true, you know, what patients say about never being left alone for two minutes together. I didn't notice it so much last time, probably because I felt much worse. Anyway, in this place, after the main round, along they all come separately, at least twice a day. Can't think why we haven't been interrupted already. They haven't done their evening rounds yet. There are about six dozen people due to work their way through this room in the next couple of hours.'

'Stiff notice on the door,' Adam said laconically. 'Leo thought you were getting a bit fractious. Said it would be a good plan for us to have a quiet talk, uninterrupted.'

Michael stared. 'Leo's incredible, you know,' he said. 'He always notices how you are feeling before you know it yourself. That's what makes him so bloody good, apart from his surgical skill, which is quite something in itself.'

'He's taken Jane to dinner, so she won't be coming in either.'

218

There was a sudden silence.

'He's in love with Jane, you know.'

'Is he?' Adam had not known this, began searching his mind for what he'd said about Jane and Michael. Had he been tactless?

'I thought you knew.'

'No. It hadn't occurred to me.'

'I never ought to have got involved with her. I ought to have left it clear for Leo. I couldn't do it. But I should have done.'

'You tried, Mike. I saw you trying.'

'Not hard enough. If I'd kept out of the way, she and Leo–' his face twisted, and he stopped.

'You're a nut case, Mike,' Adam said easily. 'You can't hand the girl about like a parcel, after all. She has some say in the problem. She's a human being, with her own instincts and affections. And rights. Including the right to make her own decisions.'

'That's what she says herself. But all I've brought her is worry and anxiety, Adam. She could have been enjoying life, having a good time.'

'Look, Mike, are you under the impression that had you turned a cold shoulder to the girl, she'd now be cosily in love with Leo? And what would be the stupendous reward, in this mythical situation? Obviously you believe in it, though personally I can't credit it for a moment.'

'She would have had peace of mind. That's

what I've destroyed.' He shook his head. 'Unforgivable, and not what I intended at all.'

'Peace of mind?' Adam repeated. 'Peace of mind, Mike? Oh no.' He was sure of this. 'You don't have peace of mind at twenty-four. I'm not sure you're even meant to have it. Youth isn't for enjoying peace of mind. None of us had it either, or wanted it. Cast your own mind back, you poor old man of thirty. I can't imagine that you ever expected or thought about peace of mind in your early twenties. Eh?'

'No, I suppose I didn't,' Michael admitted.

'None of us did. You want something for Jane, that you'd still turn down for yourself, too – careering off climbing mountains in Nepal is what caused all this trouble. Was that for peace of mind?'

Michael had to grin.

Adam changed the subject. 'Leo thinks you'll be ready for discharge next weekend,' he said.

'Good.'

'So I'll collect you on Saturday afternoon.'

'Collect me?'

'Unless Jane's free to drive you, of course. But you're coming down to Harbor's Eye, Mike, to convalesce. I take that for granted, and we both want you to. Catherine's looking forward to having you again.'

'It's very nice of you both. I was going to

stay in Harley Street for a bit.'

'No. Not suitable. With the greatest respect to your grandmother, of course. But no.'

'I'd be relieved not to. Much rather come to Halchester with you. Thanks very much, Adam.'

The following Saturday Adam collected a thin, pale and distinctly wobbly Michael, impeccably dressed in a quiet lightweight suit with a white shirt and a Central tie. Adam eyed the outfit with appreciation, managed not to comment. Instead he hoisted the familiar case, and they set off. Michael came very slowly, with his stick, for once walking, as he so often asserted he did, like an old man. Each step he took put a strain on his battered back muscles, and his operation scar was pulling painfully. He walked badly, swinging his leg clumsily in a fashion that would have made Adam shout at him a month earlier.

At Harbor's Eye, it was the close of a perfect summer's day. Catherine awaited them, with lemon tea and long chairs on the terrace.

'This is what I've been looking forward to,' Michael told her. 'All of it. This place itself is a benison.'

The sun was low in a cloudless sky, the ebb was on, the cry of the curlew echoed over the mud flats, while a cool fresh breeze came in off the distant sea to ruffle lavender and roses. Peace dropped from above, with the scents of evening. The Central was suddenly a long way away, and he was glad of it.

'It's great to be here,' he said, and stretched cautiously.

Adam was watching him. 'Bed for you in a few minutes,' he said. 'Supper in bed.'

'Supper out here.'

'No. Bed first.'

'I daresay you're right. I certainly haven't the energy to argue with you.'

'You were right,' he admitted later. 'I'm flaked out.' He was lying on his back contemplating Adam at the foot of the bed. 'A gammy back as well as no leg can be extraordinarily fatiguing, I must say. However, nothing for me to do now but lie around and recuperate. It's great to be here,' he said again. 'And to know that at last it's all behind me.' Then the sedative Adam had given him began to take effect, and he dropped off to sleep.

The next weekend Jane appeared, found Michael looking a little transparent still, and easily exhausted. She made no demands. Leo had warned her. 'Don't overpower 'im, duckie, even with love and affection. 'E'll be tired out, don't forget. And don't bully 'im about marriage, either. It's always nice to know you're wanted, of course, but 'e's grasped that by now. Not slow in the uptake, Mike. Remember 'e'll be gettin' pain from 'is back muscles still. Just be there. That'll be enough. Take it easy, and let Mike take it easy, too.' Afterwards Leo had examined himself suspiciously. How much of that little homily had been in Michael's interests, and how much in his own?

Whatever his motives had been, his advice was taken. Jane lay very low.

A fortnight later when she went down to Harbor's Eye again, she saw the difference in Michael immediately. He had been walking the cliffs with Catherine, had had a couple of sails with Adam, and when he was supposed to be lying on the terrace resting he was in fact to be found reviewing for the Diploma in Child Health, which he proposed to take in a month's time. He might put in a surgical locum first, he told the startled Jane.

'But–'

'I need to find out exactly what I'm fit for. Personally I feel as if I could push over a house. That exhaustion that's been hanging around for so long has completely gone. But there's a job coming up here in October, and I want it.'

'Here?' Jane was not only startled now, but disturbed. With Michael fit and practicing again, she had imagined them marrying and living in London. Her first registrar's post at the Central was looming into view very satisfactorily.

'Yes. In the pediatric unit at St Mark's. I'm sure I shall be fit for it by the time it comes up, and I'm pretty certain I can land it, with the appropriate support, which I've been promised.'

'Oh.' Jane digested this.

Michael saw her closed expression and read her thoughts as easily as though she had spoken them. His own face was blank, the blue eyes hooded. He had foreseen exactly what might happen. But this made it no easier to take.

Adam had been firm. If Michael was going to take on full-time surgery again, he must not attempt it in London. City life would be bad for him, on the one hand, and the demands of surgery in the Central would be too exhausting, at least for his first post after his illness. 'It's going to be all you can do, with only one leg and your recent medical history, to hold down the job here. No Central post, no city life for you, m'lad. Quiet country weekends, open air and sailing. May sound an old-fashioned regime, but it'll work.'

Michael knew he was right. But he was sure Jane ought not to throw up her own career at the Central to come down to Halchester and look after him. He was no invalid, he needed no looking after. No sacrifices were going to be made on his behalf. Giving Jane no opportunity to argue, he began discussing an article about a new and complicated series of surgical procedures for children with spina bifida. In order not to be hopelessly lost in a maze of technical and neurological detail, she had to give the account her full attention.

Catherine and Adam watched them both throughout the weekend, said nothing. On Sunday night Jane went back to London.

'She was looking very dishy,' Adam remarked. 'But I rather think he fobbed her off.'

'So do I.'

'Sandy will be back from New Zealand next week. Then we shall see.'

11

A Surgeon's Life

When Sandy came down to Halchester, he made a suggestion that put every other consideration out of Adam's mind.

'I'm retiring in October, as you may have heard.'

'Yes, Leo was talking about it.' Adam remembered what Leo had said, too. Sandy had no life apart from surgery. What was he going to do with his retirement? His thoughts were on this problem, when he heard Sandy say something that jerked him upright. He couldn't have heard him correctly. *'What?'*

'Don't look so astonished. You heard me all right. I said, how would you like to take my place?'

Adam stared at Sandy. He said nothing, but two tiny points of light behind his eyes grew and flared, until he became practically incandescent.

'You don't need to answer. I can see how you feel about it. Mike was right.'

'But – but I – how–'

'If you want the post, I don't think there'd be any obstacle. I've been sounding out opinion, and Mike hasn't been idle, either. You've been up and down to the Central a good deal in the last few years. Most people who matter have talked to you recently.'

They had indeed. It was at this point that Adam saw it all. He'd known he was under scrutiny of course. But he'd assumed that it was for past sins, not a vetting for a future post.

'Old Mummery's in favor. That's half the battle.'

'If you're in favor yourself–'

'Oh, I'd like to see you back at the Central – and there's no one I'd sooner hand over to.'

Adam's color flared as swiftly now as it would have done in his youth, Sandy saw. He felt affectionately disposed, satisfied with his arrangements. 'That's all right, then,' he said, patted him on the shoulder. 'We'll start the wheels turning, and you can put in an application. Mummery and I will be your referees. You'd better have one of the younger men, too. Perhaps Northiam. Yes, I think probably Northiam might be useful. There won't be any opposition from the juniors. Entirely the contrary. Mike's been busy, and you seem to have made an impression on Rosenstein. What he says goes with the young.'

'I like Leo,' Adam said faintly, his mind in turmoil.

'He likes you. Said so. Can work with you, were his actual words. From Leo that means a lot. Yes, he's a good lad, and talented. Worth two of Northiam, if you ask me. Though Northiam's reputation is justifiably high, of course. A pity he remains so inhuman.'

'Always been a right bastard.'

Sandy stiffened. Expressions like this had made Adam unpopular once. He hadn't changed, though the climate at the Central had. A remark of that nature would pass unnoticed there today.

'He's to be your colleague,' he said curtly. After all, he hadn't abdicated yet. 'You owe him some moderation of language, in my opinion, whatever your personal feelings.'

Adam grinned. 'I'll behave,' he promised.

That night, in some trepidation, he told Catherine, who had lived in Halchester all her life, loved and knew the countryside and the people. 'I should never have accepted without consulting you,' he said. 'It means moving to London, a total change in our way of life. And I just said yes without waiting to find out what you thought about it.' He was beginning to feel very uneasy about this.

'Of course you did,' Catherine said at once. She surveyed him, humor and affection in her glance. 'You've been bouncing about all evening, all lit up. I knew it must be something important.' She put her arms around him. 'Oh Adam, it's your dream. You never believed it could come true. But it has. Oh darling, I'm so thankful.' Her eyes were wet.

'Hey – crying? You don't want to go.' His voice was stunned.

'Darling, it's not that at all. I'm just so *pleased*.'

Adam remained unconvinced. *'Crying?'* he repeated.

'I'm so happy for you,' Catherine explained.

Adam shook his head. He was baffled. But it seemed to be all right. He took her hand. 'Anyway, you'll come?' he asked, beginning to swing it confidently. 'We'll look for a house?'

They were still looking for one, and staying with Lady Adversane in Harley Street, when the date for Sandy's retirement finally arrived. He had been at the Central for over forty years. There was to be a big party in the orthopedic unit the following day, but tonight his former registrars – or as many of them as were within reach of London – were giving him dinner and making a presentation. The affair was arranged by Leo. Only five years had gone by since he had been Sandy's registrar, and though he had made it now onto the staff of the Central, he was one of the youngest present. Adam, for

230

instance, had left over fifteen years earlier. His appointment as Sandy's successor had been announced a month ago, and he had already begun work in the orthopedic unit.

'Yes, I remember Trowbridge,' one of the arrivals from the north of England agreed. 'He was newly qualified when I left – a bit of a firebrand, we thought then.'

'Oh yeah, I reckon 'e remains a bit of a firebrand,' Leo said.

Someone else joined them. 'I hear Trowbridge is taking over. I used to know him quite well at one time. Must say, I never expected to see him on the staff.'

'Don't think 'e did either,' Leo commented.

'But then I never expected to see you on it, Leo. And there you are, they tell me, on Mummery's firm and doing very well for yourself, while I vegetate out at Bletchley. I don't understand it.' The speaker raised astonished eyebrows, but the eyes beneath shone with laughter. He understood it very well.

'What I don't understand about Trowbridge,' a third speaker observed, 'is why he's had the opportunity. I thought the place was being kept warm for young Adversane. Sandy's godson, and a very promising surgeon when I last saw him. I know I must be out of touch...' his voice dwindled in the arctic silence which had overtaken him. 'Has

Adversane made off with the family silver, then? Or eloped to the States with a bird?'

'Nothing like that,' Leo said. 'I'm surprised you 'aven't 'eard, though.'

'Heard what?'

Leo told him.

'What an abominable thing to happen. How is he?'

'Judge for yourself. 'Ere 'e is.' He looked across to where Michael's back could be seen, talking to Sandy, who was summoning a waiter and proffering drinks.

'Is that Adversane? What a conservative back view he presents nowadays – when I last saw him, he almost had his hair in ringlets, and his evening attire consisted of velvet and ruffles, as far as I remember. Mind you, it was some years ago. But that's an exceptionally traditional back, wouldn't you say?'

'Dark dinner jacket, faultless it looks from here, hair off the collar. I suppose you're sure it is Adversane?'

'Of course it is, Bill. Six foot two or so, narrow shoulders, long legs, dark curls and that tilt to the head. There you are.' Michael had turned, was scanning the scene. He raised a hand to Leo, made his way over. 'Hi, Leo.'

'Hi, matey. You look very fit.'

'I am.'

'So you've landed that job at St Mark's?'

'That's right. I'm enjoying it. What's more,

I can actually do it quite adequately. Junior consultant in general surgery in the Pediatric Unit. I started a week ago – the same day that Adam took over at the Central, as it happens.'

Leo's gaze had switched. He was counting heads. 'Everyone seems to be 'ere now,' he announced. 'So I think I'll just check on the table. See if they're ready for us.'

'I'll come with you.'

They went through into the dining room together.

Eyes followed them. 'I thought there was meant to be a feud between those two?' the man from Bletchley commented. 'There certainly was in my time.'

'Oh no. That's out of date. Thick as thieves these days.'

'Adversane walks very well, considering.'

'He does, doesn't he? Looks sturdy, too, allowing for the fact that when he was first admitted here from Nepal we all thought we'd need to be damn lucky not to lose him.' This was Robbie Pollock, Sandy's present registrar, and the youngest in the room. He looked through the door to where Leo's broad back and Michael's slim one could be seen conferring with the wine waiter. 'Those are two nice blokes,' he said. 'You couldn't do better.'

The two nice blokes settled the wine and turned, on their way back to the main group.

'By the way,' Leo said. 'Adam's taking the foot of the table and I'm joining 'im at that end, with Robbie. Sandy wants you next to 'im at the other end, and the senior member of the party – that's Murray-Browne from Leeds. 'E was 'is first registrar, 'e says, when 'e came onto the staff.'

'Don't know him.'

'Nor me.'

'Leo,' Michael said abruptly.

Leo gave him a sharp, wary glance. 'It's all right, I know,' he said. 'Madam told me.'

'I–'

'Ferget it.'

'Well–'

'Pack it in, mate. I wanna get them to the table. If they go on standin' about like this we'll be all night.'

So dinner began.

It ended with the presentation to Sandy. This was not exactly a surprise, though he had affected to be unaware of the purpose of numerous long-winded conversations both Robbie Pollock and Leo, then finally Adam had engaged him in, on the subject of what luxury he would buy if money was no object. The answer, now it saw the light of day, proved to be a small Persian rug in tawny reds and soft greens. 'Just what I wanted,' Sandy exclaimed, his eyes alight with mingled pleasure and humor. 'How did you all guess?'

'I wouldn't describe it quite as guessin',' Leo observed.

'More in the nature of "ascertaining,"' Robbie Pollock suggested. There was a bellow of laughter around the table, this being a favorite Drummond word.

Then came the demands for 'speech.'

Sandy produced an envelope, consulted it. 'Oddly enough, I did happen to make a few jottings,' he confided. 'In case, by some strange coincidence...' his words died away in shouts. A few extroverted individuals banged the table, and Sandy launched into thanks, personal reminiscences – verging often on the libellous – of each of them in undisciplined youth. Then, finally, 'And so what am I going to do with myself?' he demanded.

No one answered him. This was the question they had all been asking. 'What on earth is the dear old boy going to do with himself?'

'I'll tell you. Marry off m'daughter.' He looked them over smugly, allowing his eye to roam ostentatiously up one side of the table and down the other, until it finally, along with every other eye, came to rest on an apprehensive Michael Adversane. 'Yes, I'm glad to be able to make an announcement. You'll see it in the paper tomorrow anyway. My daughter Jane – whom all of you know, but not all of you may realize is now qualified and working on the Professional Medical Unit–' more applause. The Drummond party was becoming distinctly rowdy '–is marrying Michael Adversane next month.' He looked around the assembly again. 'Mike's had to face some major surgery, as most of you know by now. Some of you, of course, have been involved in caring for him.'

'I wouldn't describe you as exactly uninvolved yourself,' Michael pointed out. 'If you hadn't flown out to Nepal at half an hour's notice, more or less, and resuscitated me, I reckon I wouldn't be here now.'

Sandy gave him an affectionate smile. 'We couldn't do without you, Jane and I,' he said, blew his nose. 'Now, I don't know if Mike has told you he's back in surgery, working down at Halchester. Adam Trowbridge – who, as you all undoubtedly ascertained long before this, is taking my place in the Orthopedic Unit – is selling Mike and Jane his house, Harbor's Eye. And that's where I propose to spend a large portion of my time in the future, interfering in the upbringing of my grandchildren.'

This was only what he had said earlier to Michael. 'Marry the girl, let her make a career for herself down at St Mark's with you, Mike. It's what she wants. She's given her heart to you, and she's yours. No one can take your place.'

Michael caught his breath. It was the truth.

'She began to love you in the nursery, and she's never altered. Giving up a post in the Central is nothing by comparison.'

Michael remained dubious.

'Love the girl, don't you?' Sandy demanded. 'Or have I got it wrong?'

'Of course I love her. Have done for years. Perhaps I began in the nursery too, without knowing it. Certainly I've never felt like this about anyone else. Never.'

'Then tell her so, damn it.'

So at last he did just that, in the garden at Harbor's Eye one afternoon in September, the late sun setting over the water, the familiar cry of the curlew in their ears.

'I must say it's nice to hear it at last,' was all Jane said, though her wide radiant smile and the brilliance of her eyes told him more. 'Goodness knows I've proposed to you often enough,' she added. 'It would serve you right if I told you this wasn't the moment, let you sweat it out for a while. But I shan't risk it.' She flung her arms around him, as she had so often done before. But this time he made no attempt to disengage himself.

The publishers hope that this book has given you enjoyable reading. Large Print Books are especially designed to be as easy to see and hold as possible. If you wish a complete list of our books please ask at your local library or write directly to:

Dales Large Print Books
Magna House, Long Preston,
Skipton, North Yorkshire.
BD23 4ND